RANGER KNOX

- SHIFTER NATION -

WEREBEARS OF ACADIA

MEG RIPLEY

MEG RIPLEY

Ranger Knox
Copyright © 2017 by Meg Ripley
www.redlilypublishing.com

All rights reserved. Printed in the United States of America. No part of this book may be used or reproduced in any manner whatsoever without written permission except in the case of brief quotations embodied in critical articles or reviews.

This book is a work of fiction. Names, characters, businesses, organizations, places, events and incidents either are the product of the authors' imagination or are used fictitiously. Any resemblance to actual persons, living or dead, events, or locales is entirely coincidental.

Disclaimer

This book is intended for readers age 18 and over. It contains mature situations and language that may be objectionable to some readers.

First Edition: September 2017

TABLE OF CONTENTS

CHAPTER ONE	4
CHAPTER TWO	14
CHAPTER THREE	26
CHAPTER FOUR	36
CHAPTER FIVE	48
CHAPTER SIX	58
CHAPTER SEVEN	72
CHAPTER EIGHT	80
CHAPTER NINE	91
CHAPTER TEN	110
CHAPTER ELEVEN	120
CHAPTER TWELVE	131
CHAPTER THIRTEEN	145
CHAPTER FOURTEEN	156
ABOUT THE AUTHOR	172

CHAPTER ONE
HANNAH

I pull into the spot where my Airbnb host said I could leave my car and look around me. It's my first time in Bar Harbor, and though my surroundings look more beautiful than anything I've ever seen on the Travel Channel, I'm not here to admire the foliage: I have an ulterior motive. Sure, the magazine could force me to use my vacation time, but they couldn't keep me from writing while I did.

I've been trying to work my way up to a full-time editorial position with *New World* for about a year, and when HR told me that I had to either take my vacation time or lose it, I hatched a plan to work on something while I was away. The magazine has its one-thousandth issue coming out in a month, and I figured--I hoped--that an exposé on the controversial history behind the National Park Service would put me in a better position to get ahead. So, I scheduled my vacation time and booked an Airbnb in Bar Harbor, a quaint little tourist town right outside of Maine's Acadia National Park, and started to plan my research.

    I'd gotten the idea from a piece I'd read recently, which delved into how the National Park Service came into existence. Of course, there had always been green spaces that rich people bought up and set aside as conservation areas, but there was something in the article about the founders--something I couldn't put my finger on--that struck me as a little odd. Aside from that, I'd come across these wacko conspiracy theory websites claiming the national parks were actually set up for some kind of nefarious purpose. The theories I'd read speculated they were being used as reserves for fossil fuels or gold and other precious metals; the most interesting and least likely to be true theory was that the lands had been set aside by freemasons and other occult groups in power for the sake of performing secret ceremonies.

I grab my laptop case and backpack off the passenger seat and check my phone to make sure I'm on time. Mary, the woman whose house I'm staying in, seems to be a fairly accommodating host, based on the messages we've been exchanging, anyway. Her place is more accessible than the hotels in Bar Harbor, and considering it's the height of foliage season, much cheaper. I lock my car out of habit, even though I can't imagine anyone on the sleepy little street stealing from me.

It's chillier than I thought it would be, so I hurry up to the front door of the little house, pulling my denim jacket tight around me. I knock on the door and wait, fidgeting as I look around. Maine is one of those places that's stunning when you're looking at it in pictures or video, but if you're standing outside in late September, it's chilly and damp, making it hard to appreciate the beauty of the yellow, orange, and red leaves on the trees.

"You must be Hannah!" Mary looks like someone's mom: gray-streaked chestnut hair, wrinkles at the corners of her eyes, wearing a matching pink sweatsuit with 80s-era floral appliques stitched on the chest and pant legs. "Quick, come inside, dear; it's getting cold out there."

I follow her through the door and make small talk about my drive up as she gives me a tour of the house. The kitchen has plenty of cast iron and a gas-powered stove--according to Mary, it's more reliable than electric in the winters. Mary leads me upstairs to my room, explaining about the bathroom and how she got a tankless, gas-powered water heater installed so that she'd never have to wait for hot water.

She shows me to the guest room, giving me the chance to unpack and get settled, but instead, I pull out my laptop and search for the Acadia National Park website. I chose it as the place for my work-cation because Acadia was one of the first national parks established by the NPS; I'd hoped it would be a good place to start.

I look over the material I've already assembled about the park, thinking about how I'll kick off my investigation. *Well, the first thing to do would be to get there and check the place out,* I decide as I examine the maps of the area. Mary's place is about two miles away--close enough that, in theory, I could walk there, but if I did, I may not have enough energy left to explore the place. It's taken me all day to get up to Maine and it's already late afternoon; I should probably wait until the morning, but if I want to get a real feel for the place, I'm going to need to check it out when there aren't as many visitors there. I change into some warmer clothes--a thicker pair of jeans, a turtleneck sweater and a beanie--and I tell Mary that I'm off to run some errands.

I get back into my car and pull up the directions to the park. I've got about another hour or so before it's too dark to really see, but I've got a heavy flashlight with me, so I'm not too worried.

As I pull into the park a few minutes later, I fumble through the glove compartment in search of the one-week pass I'd ordered online before my trip and hand it to the ranger at the gate. I take a second look and have to admit he's pretty hot; he fills out that uniform really well with those broad shoulders of his. His deep brown hair and beard are cut short, and he's got strikingly bright green eyes.

"Just to let you know, the visitor center is closed for the day, but the park is open twenty-four hours," he tells me. "If you need any help, there are signs posted just about everywhere telling you how to get in touch with the rangers."

"Thanks," I tell him, taking back my visitor pass. Maybe I can interview him about Acadia, or at least get an official quote.

"I'm on duty for the rest of night, so I'll be checking to make sure that everyone gets out. If you plan on staying late, give me a call up here at the gate and I'll keep folks from coming after you to make sure you're not dead or lost," he says with a little smile.

I grin back at him. "That seems normal," I say, not quite sarcastic. "Give me the number, and I'll be sure to let you know that I'm okay." I program the number into my phone and the ranger passes me through the gate, heading back to the warmth of the guard house while I pull forward.

I don't see many cars in the lot, but that makes sense; it's starting to get dark, and it's chilly, too-- enough so that I'm glad I thought to change into warmer clothes. I grab my flashlight and make sure I've got my phone and a few other things in my purse, and climb out of the car.

As I'm walking towards one of the hiking trails, I have to admit, the park is genuinely beautiful. It's almost the end of the foliage season, and I could see why outdoorsy people would come to the park at the peak of it. I step onto the path and breathe in the scent of dried leaves, loamy soil, and the shoreline, trying to get a feel for everything around me.

I start wandering, falling into a kind of rhythm that helps me to think. It'll be easier to get more intel when it's daylight, but as night begins to fall around me, there's something about the quiet of the place that makes it a little easier to understand why people might conjure up all these bizarre theories.

Right then, something shifts in the air, and I get the sense that I'm being watched, but I can't see anyone when I look around to prove it to myself. Even though I've been a journalist for a few years, I've never really been in any kind of dangerous situation before; there's no reason anyone would be after me, anyway. Right?

The deeper I get into the wooded areas around the hiking trail, the more the eerie feeling starts to weigh on me. Maybe it's just campers or rangers working, but a primal part of me feels like there's something else at play.

Something predatory.

I try to remain calm by reminding myself there aren't all that many predators in this area; black bears and coyotes are out here, but they're shy, and I have to assume they're not all that interested in attacking humans.

"Shake it off, they're more afraid of you than you are of them," I tell myself, looking around. I realize that I'm on a loop, and decide that instead of branching off onto one of the more remote trails, I'll just move ahead and make my way back to the parking lot.

Just then, I hear the distinct sound of a stick breaking behind me, followed by what sounds like a growl.

My heart starts pounding in my chest. "Probably just a coyote going after a rabbit or something," I tell myself as I start to move a little faster on the path, trying to get back to my car as quickly as possible.

I hear something else, something I can't even name; a sound I don't even know the word for, and that's enough to make me launch into a steady jog. It's dark, and though my flashlight is shaking uncontrollably in my hand, there's still enough light for me to see the path ahead of me. I hear more movement behind me, and despite telling myself that it's probably nothing, or that I'm just overreacting to the darkness and the creepy silence of the woods, I start sprinting outright.

"Get her!"

That is something I absolutely can't mistake for being some coyote or bobcat going after prey in the underbrush. I can't be certain it's directed at me, but it seems like the best idea is to just get the hell out of there as fast as I can, no matter who it's actually directed at.

I nearly make it to the trail's entrance when I hear the heavy footfalls right behind me, faster than I would have imagined possible, and I stumble over some uneven patch of the trail and land on the damp ground below with a thud.

"Fuck!" I mutter, struggling to get back on my feet to flee. I can't lie to myself for a second longer; there's someone--or some*thing*--chasing me, and I need to get to my car. What the hell ever possessed me to think it was a good idea to visit this park and hike these trails alone at night?

CHAPTER TWO
KNOX

Some of those new assholes are chasing after a park visitor!

The words ring out in my brain almost like a shout, and I recognize the mental "voice" of one of the members of my clan, Cassidy Powers. I put her on trail duty for the night, and when I reach out to her mind, I can place her close to one of the easier hiking paths.

I've been waiting for those bastards to do something I can call them out on for the last three weeks. Since Acadia is neutral territory for shifters, I can't kick them out--even as an Alpha--unless I have good reason to, and catching them committing a crime should be reason enough. I start heading in the direction I can feel Cassidy's signal coming from, and I keep my ears open for any hint of what the pricks might be doing.

I slow down a bit once I get onto the right trail, taking a few moments to catch my breath. Just ahead of me, I catch the tail end of one of them running along the trail. My heart beats faster in my chest for reasons that have nothing to do with running and I growl to myself, thinking of how I'd like to call those fucking pissants out formally and take them down.

Instead, I have to deal with the situation at hand. I vaguely catch the scent of a human female overlaid by the mark of the four bears chasing her. If these guys are going after a *human* park visitor, that's a big problem, and one I'm going to have to take care of as neatly as possible. They didn't even bother shifting into their bear forms; at least if they had, I could publicly dismiss it as a random wildlife incursion.

As I pursue the group and their prey, I start thinking of how I'm going to handle brushing this incident aside. There was some chick from a magazine calling the park a week or so before, and based on her questioning, I have a feeling she was priming the pump to uncover some things that are better left alone. And if word gets out that there's been an attack on someone visiting the park, there's no way she'll keep it out of whatever bullshit article she's working on.

I catch up to the group just before the entrance to the trails, and I hear the woman, who's now shouting.

"Don't think you're going to get anything from me--not without a goddamn fight!"

I can't help but be a bit impressed by her feisty spirit, and as I try to sneak up on them, I catch little glimpses of her as they follow her deeper into the woods. I assume they're probably planning to steal whatever valuables she's got on her--or maybe, do worse.

The woman must have taken some kind of self-defense classes; she stopped running and is now kicking and throwing punches, turning her head to bite as viciously as any cornered animal would, making it tough for her would-be attackers to get what they want from her.

"Let's take her to the campsite. Knock her out, Kevin."

"What the fuck? This was supposed to be a quick grab, Shawn. Let's just get her purse and get out of here, man. Right, Harris? Jamie?"

Shawn leers at the woman, "Yeah, but she's a hot little piece..."

I let them hear me approach, crunching hard on some underbrush and sticks to announce myself.

"You have two seconds to get the hell out of here," I say, letting the Alpha growl reverberate through my voice. There's one benefit to these interlopers not being part of my clan: they couldn't hear me coming, since they aren't tuned into the same telepathic channel.

"Oh, shit," I hear one of them mutter.

"Uh, we were just *helping* this young lady find her way back to her car," Jamie stammers, but he knows I'm not buying any of his bullshit.

"Did I stutter?" I get in his face and roar, "Get the fuck out of here. Now!"

Shawn, their Alpha, tries to posture a bit, but after a moment, with a low growl, they slink away into the woods. In the distance, I recognize the faint sounds of them shifting into their bear forms as they proceed to lumber off and sulk.

My focus shifts to the next priority: taking care of the woman, who is now sitting on a nearby boulder.

"You okay? I tried to get here before they could do anything," I say.

"Just got a good scare," she says. I move closer to her and see that she's managed to hold onto her purse; points for that, I guess. During the chase, I'd been too obsessed with getting to her before the outsiders could do anything, but now that we're close--and the adrenaline is starting to ebb out of my system--I can actually appreciate the scent of her; it reminds me of lavender honey, fresh out of a hive deep in the woods, and I recognize it as the scent of the visitor I'd just given the office phone number to an hour or so ago. I inhale once again;

my mouth begins to water, but as I start to pick up on the sharper smell of her fear and anger, I have to remind myself she was almost the victim of an attack; one that could jeopardize the secrecy of Acadia.

"Here, let me help you up," I offer, reaching out to give her a hand. Even with my keen eyesight, in the dark, it's hard to make out too many particulars, but I can tell she's got an incredible body beneath her clothes: full breasts and round hips with a little padding along her thighs that triggers vivid images of what it'd be like to have those sexy legs wrapped around me. She doesn't accept my hand, but instead, rises from her seat on the huge chunk of granite and dusts herself off.

"Thanks for coming to my rescue," she says blandly.

"Just doing my job," I tell her, giving her a smile that I'm pretty sure her human eyes can't see in the darkness of the forest. "Please, let me walk you to your car to make sure you get out of here alright."

"I guess you could do that," the woman says, shifting her purse on her shoulder.

"What are you up to, wandering the woods at night, anyway?" We take off in the direction of the trail out to the parking lot, and I'm doing my best to get answers, while seeming to make small talk along the way.

"I know--I was actually heading back to my car when they started chasing me," the woman says. "I guess I just wanted to do a quick trip through a bit of the park before I settle further into my research."

"Research? Are you a scientist?" I haven't received any petitions for studies, but sometimes students do trips on their own, without grants or funding, for papers. The woman I'm walking with doesn't look like she's much older than the average grad student, so that could be the case.

"I'm a journalist, actually," she tells me. "I'm investigating the history of the National Park Service for an article, and I wanted to get a feel for one of its parks before starting to delve deeper, so I planned a little trip up here to Acadia."

I nearly stop dead in my tracks.

"A journalist?" *Great. Of course those assholes chose literally the worst person to attack.* This is going to make things even more complicated.

"Yeah—I'm working with *New World* magazine," she says. "The name's Hannah Grant." She holds out her hand for me to shake it, and I oblige, in spite of the multiple distractions raging for control of my mind.

"Knox Bernard," I tell her. "We've spoken before." I see her eyes widen as we pass into the lighted area surrounding the parking lot.

"You're the administrator for this park," she says, looking at me sharply. "We talked on the phone."

"We did," I agree. *God could this situation get worse?*

"You're...much more attractive than you sounded on the phone," the woman says, smiling a little awkwardly.

"I don't know if I should be offended or flattered," I tell her. She laughs, and it's like someone's run a finger down my spine in the best way possible.

"No, I didn't mean it as an insult at all," she says, shaking her head. "I'm just surprised that you're the one who came to my rescue, I guess." She shakes her head again and rummages through her purse. "I should probably head back to my Airbnb before I embarrass myself even more."

"Let me just check you over before you leave," I suggest, partly because I want to make sure she's actually okay, but also because I want an excuse to linger. The scent rolling off her is enough to drive me mad; aside from that, I have to set some ground rules about this article she's working on. I can't be having a scandalous investigation into the park underway.

"I guess," Hannah says, looking at me warily. I hold up my flashlight and wave the light over her hands, up her arms and down her legs, checking her over. I don't really need it--there's enough light from the moon and the safety lamps set out in the parking lot for me to see clearly--but it gives me an excuse to take my time, and besides: she doesn't need to know that I can already see her as plain as day.

"I hope that little incident didn't give you a bad first impression of the park," I say, playing the light over her back. Her denim jacket must have gotten snagged on something; but thankfully, it's not torn through.

"Well, it certainly gave me a good first impression of the park *rangers*," Hannah says playfully. "Rushing to help this stupid damsel in distress."

"It could've happened to anyone," I tell her. "I've been trying to run those campers out of here for a couple of weeks, but they're paid up and I haven't had anything I can use as leverage 'til now. Hopefully this changes things."

"You know who they were?"

"I know this park inside and out," I point out with a little smile. "Well, you look like you're all in one piece, but you should check yourself over for ticks once you get back home."

"I will," Hannah says. And then we're just standing there in the parking lot, awkwardly, with maybe a foot and a half of space between us. "Are you on duty tomorrow? I was hoping I could get a tour...in the daylight, of course."

"I'm off duty, technically," I reply, thinking fast. "But if you want to get a tour of the park, I'd be more than happy to show you around."

"That would be great," Hannah says.

"Think you can get here at about two? It should be warm enough, and we can make good time along the shoreline and through the wooded areas."

"You realize I'm going to be interviewing you," Hannah says, making it not quite a question.

"I expected as much," I say, grinning at her. "Two?"

"That works," she tells me, smiling back. "Thanks again. For...you know."

"Just doing my job," I insist. I turn away from her, stepping back to watch the gentle swaying of her hips as she walks the rest of the way to her car. I'm not sure whether I'm looking forward to tomorrow because it'll give me a chance to run interference, or to be around that lingering, sweet scent of hers, but I can only hope I can get enough sleep to be functional before I have to meet up with her.

I watch as her car pulls away and then head back onto the trail, towards the part of the woods where the interlopers disappeared to. I'm going to have to discuss the incident with the members of my clan, and if I expect to be able to expel these bastards from the neutral, sacred lands of the park, I'll need some solid evidence to present to the conclave of shifters.

CHAPTER THREE
HANNAH

The morning after my ill-fated trip to Acadia National Park, I'm up early, scanning through some of the research I've already done, trying to put together a cohesive strategy for interviewing Knox Bernard later in the day.

As I look through my records, there's something odd I keep coming across, and while it doesn't make me feel like I'm becoming a full-on conspiracy theorist, it does set off some red flags. Like many of the national parks that exist in the US, Acadia was made possible through lots of advocacy and generous contributions from wealthy men--but the donations were made by the same handful of families repeatedly.

Most well-off families do benevolent things to get their names in history books. But a lot of the people involved in the establishment of Acadia, and the National Park Service as a whole, seemed to not want any credit at all. I decide by around eleven that I'll ask Knox what he knows about the history of the park itself, and start getting ready for our meeting. I've got a few bumps and bruises from falling on the trail, but I'm actually surprised at how unafraid I am to venture back into the woods. Of course, that could just be because I won't be alone, and especially because the ranger who'll be taking me around is actually pretty hot.

I weave my hair into a french braid and pull an old cap from my university over my head to keep the sun out of my eyes. It's cool enough that it makes perfect sense to wear hiking boots, my other pair of thick jeans, and a heavy pullover sweater. I find myself hoping that I at least look halfway decent; not that I should be worried about how I look, other than needing to come across as professional.

"Headed out to the park? It looks like a beautiful day for a hike," Mary says as I clomp downstairs from my room.

"Yeah. I'm even getting a special tour," I tell her. I'd mentioned I was going to be in town to work on an article for *New World*, but I hadn't given away any details about what I was actually investigating, just that the piece is about national parks in general.

"Oh really? Well a cute young thing like you is bound to get some special treatment," Mary says, pouring herself another cup of coffee. "Want me to fix you up some of this in a thermos? It'll help to keep you warm out there."

"I'd love some. Thanks," I say, smiling at her.

I check over everything in my bag as she's hustling about the kitchen to get my thermos ready: I've got my recorder, a spare microphone, a notepad with some preliminary questions written out, a heavy-duty flashlight, a full bottle of water, my phone, maps and guides of the park--everything

I need for the day's trek and for the interview I lined up with Knox.

I wonder absently about the guys who tried to attack me, and what's become of them, but I know I'm not going to include that detail in the article unless I absolutely have to--that's not the kind of incident I want to have my name next to, if only because it makes me look like a total idiot for putting myself in that predicament in the first place.

In no time flat, I'm pulling through the gate at Acadia. I spot Knox waiting for me, and I have to admit: in full daylight--even without his uniform--he looks super hot. He's in a pair of relaxed jeans that fit snug in all the right places, along with a shirt that looks a little light for the weather, a leather jacket, and rugged hiking boots.

I find an empty parking spot--there are a lot fewer of them now, since it's daylight--and pull into it, checking my hair and making sure I collected everything I'd need. I climb out of my car and by the time I've got it locked up and my bag slung over my shoulder, Knox is only a couple of yards away. I see him looking me over and realize that I'm not the only one who likes what they see.

"Good day for a hike," he says, giving me a smile. For a second, something vaguely primal flashes in his eyes, and I have to wonder if I imagined it somehow.

"You do know that I'm going to spend the entire time trying to pry information out of you, right?" It only seems fair to give him warning, but I give him a little smile to go with it. I'm not usually coy or all that flirty with people I'm interviewing, but there's something about Knox that makes me blush and flutter my eyelashes.

Up close, he's more muscular than I realized the night before; I can almost make out his pecs against the fabric of his shirt. He's definitely more ripped than I would imagine a park ranger to be, and I can't help, just for a second, imagining what he would look like naked.

Shit! You stop that right now, Hannah Grant. I take a quick breath to try and stifle the heat that seems to be coursing through my veins, heading just south of my hips. *What is wrong with me?*

"I expected as much," Knox says, keeping that little grin on his face. I notice something secretive in his eyes, and begin to wonder if maybe I'm onto something; perhaps some of the bizarre claims I've read about the NPS aren't so outlandish after all. I can't think of what else he could feel the need to hide, but I'll play along for now.

"Well, shall we get started?" I open the thermos and take a swig of coffee. "I've got all day, but the sooner we start…"

"The sooner we'll have it done and over with," Knox finishes for me. "Let me show you my favorite trail."

We start off in that direction and I fall into step with the ranger, running the questions through my head and trying to figure out where to begin.

"So, I'm assuming that as the manager of the park, you're pretty well-versed in its history," I say. "Oh! I almost forgot. Do you mind if I record this?"

"Not at all, go right ahead," Knox replies. I take the recorder out of my bag and rattle off my standard disclaimer, holding the machine a few inches from Knox's face for him to confirm his agreement to being recorded.

"So, as I was saying, I assume you're pretty knowledgeable about the park's history," I begin again.

"It comes with the territory," Knox says. "Is there something specific you want to know?"

"While I was doing my research, I came up sort of...confused, I guess, about some of the founders," I say. "Obviously, the main people involved were Christopher Ellsworth, his father Christopher B. Ellsworth, and Theodore Davis, but there were others too, right?"

"Of course," Knox nods. "What about them?"

"A lot of them don't seem to have much in the way of public records," I say. "I mean, there are notations that they contributed or lobbied to the cause, but when I tried to find some of their birth certificates, for example, I came up empty."

Knox shrugs. "It was nearly a century ago, so keep in mind, many of the records might be a little shoddy."

I frown at that, but I can't think of a way to press the point further. "So, Knox, you've probably heard the strange rumors about Acadia, and the National Park Service in general. What are your thoughts?" I hurry a bit to keep up with him as we head up a little incline. I have to admit it's beautiful out, even if it's a bit chilly.

"The conspiracy wackos?" Knox gives me a sardonic grin. "Don't tell me you're doing some hit piece about how the people who created the national parks were all warlocks and freemasons."

"No, no; I'm trying to do as straightforward a piece as possible," I say quickly. "But it does come up, you know."

"I know," Knox nods. "It's just always seemed so ridiculous to me--doesn't it seem that way to you?"

"Well, we know a lot of the founding fathers were masons, or members of other fraternities," I counter; I'm not even sure why I'm pressing the point at all, because a day ago, I found the whole idea ridiculous. "But obviously, the idea of building a bunch of parks to make it easier to sacrifice goats in private is a bit much to believe."

"Glad to hear you think so," Knox says, his voice rippling with amusement.

We come to a stopping point and I mention I need to sit down for a bit; I offer Knox some coffee and he waves me off. "I've actually got a picnic basket with some snacks hidden for us down the trail a bit," he tells me. "Did you bring water, too, or just coffee?"

"I have a water bottle, and it's full," I tell him, and he nods his approval.

"Do you do much hiking, Hannah?"

I shrug off the question. "Some, but my job doesn't leave me much time to."

"How did you end up in this line of work, anyway?"

"Kind of by accident," I explain. "I always liked asking questions, and I enjoyed writing back in school, so when it came time to pick a major, journalism sounded like the perfect path. By the time I graduated, I had honed my skills...and well, here I am." I take another sip of my still-warm coffee and look at Knox speculatively. "How about you? When did you decide to become a park ranger?"

"I've wanted to be one since I was a kid," Knox says. "I've always loved the outdoors; hunting, camping, fishing. I even took foraging classes when I was young. My parents liked living off the land, and when I turned twelve, we did a tour of the different national parks; that's when I decided."

I try to picture Knox as a twelve-year-old boy, foraging in the woods for mushrooms, berries or whatever, but it's impossible. He's far too masculine and fully-grown for me to imagine him any other way.

"Ready to move on?" he asks, gesturing toward the next leg of the trail.

CHAPTER FOUR
KNOX

"What can you tell me about Theodore Davis?"

I had hoped that Hannah would give up the line of questioning about the park's early history after what I'd said before, but she's obviously intent on digging deep. Of course, I can't tell her much about Davis; only the official history.

"He was a major conservationist, and a wealthy guy," I say, turning a corner and glancing back to look at Hannah.

I've been trying to stay downwind of her the entire time we've been hiking. I nearly forgot just how good she smells, and how much her scent--lavender honey, and now, after some hiking, a deeper musk that drives my animal instincts into overdrive--makes me want nothing more than to carry her off into one of the more isolated areas and explore every inch of her body. *She's not even your kind. Get your head out of the clouds.*

"He was one of several people involved in the establishment of the park. Davis donated a bunch of his land and convinced some of his rich buddies to do so as well. He was one of the guys who was able to get the area protected by the feds. The government eventually agreed to preserve the space as a monument, but it didn't get its status as a national park until after the National Park Service was formed a few years later."

"Have you heard any anecdotes explaining what spurred his interest in conservation to begin with?"

I glance at her again; Hannah's keeping pace with me pretty well, even without the advantage of having the preternatural speed that comes with being a shifter.

"Lots of rich people back then made it their pet cause, and they still do today. It's a way to preserve beautiful landscapes, and add some credit to their names. You know?"

"I guess that makes sense, but why not...I don't know. Why not build hospitals, or something like that?"

I shrug. "Some of them did that, too," I tell her. "But a lot of them liked to be in the great outdoors in their downtime, and the best way to make sure they could enjoy it was to set up parks like this one."

Of course, the real reason behind why many of the conservationists were so devoted to the cause is a very different story. One that Hannah could never know.

Davis and a handful of the other founders--his comrades--were shifters.

Around the turn of the twentieth century, the industrial revolution began to encroach on our normal safe spaces, the same way it had been pushing out other wildlife. We needed areas where we could shift at will or during the full moon; to be ourselves and embrace our dual natures while being shielded from the public eye. So, while Davis and his associates were rallying for the designation of a preserved space for us here in Maine, other wealthy shifters with political prowess infiltrated the federal government and made their case for forging the National Park Service as a whole, which would establish preservation areas for shifters across the nation.

As for Hannah, hopefully, if I keep repeating the story that's on the official record, I can get her off this line of questioning altogether. I'm pledged--as every shifter is--to keeping our kind and its history secret. Because of my position as the administrator of Acadia, as well as the Alpha of my clan, I have the responsibility of making sure no outsiders know about the real purpose behind the national parks. Hannah is most definitely an outsider, no matter how much the ursine part of my brain keeps insisting that she should belong to me.

"I guess maybe the fact that it was mostly a bunch of super-wealthy people is why some folks are so keen on the idea that they were free masons, or Elks, or whatever," Hannah says.

"People are always going to say weird things like that about rich people," I agree. *Thank god. That's an answer she can deal with.*

I'm about to change the subject when I hear the voice of one of my clan-mates, Jack, in my mind.

No one's been able to track down the four of them. We're combing the woods, but they've done something to cover their scent trail.

I almost groan out loud at the news; after I saw Hannah safely out of the park last night, I'd sent the word out to track down and capture the bears who'd tried to attack her. Since they were outsiders, no one could track them by their mental signature--they weren't attuned to the rest of us--and if they were somehow managing to cover their scent-trails, that made it even harder.

"Something wrong?" I look around and see that I've slowed down to a near-stop, and Hannah is looking up at me, concerned.

"I just remembered something," I say, shaking my head. With her so close, I can't avoid breathing in her scent, and it drives any worry about the bastards completely from my mind, replacing it with the bone-deep need to touch her. I make myself step back, away from her, and fill my lungs with some of the crisp air of the surrounding forest. "Let's keep going; the basket of food I put together for us is just ahead."

I can feel the heat flowing through my body, and just from being around Hannah, and breathing in her scent, I can already feel myself getting hard. This is disastrous. I need to get away from her as soon as I can; not just because she's distracting as hell, but because I need to find a way to deal with the bears that almost attacked her.

I send a signal to the members of my clan, telling them they need to comb back through the woods, and if they have to, raid the camp the interlopers set up for themselves amongst the cabins and find whatever they need to get a good scent-mark to go by.

We get to the spot where I put the basket off to the side and I lead Hannah out to a clearing; it's one of those places that the hikers and tourists almost never get to, because it's off the trail and a little under cover, and it's one of my favorite places in the park to visit when I'm by myself. I can't say for sure why I've brought Hannah here specifically, except that it's quiet and well-lit during the day.

"So," she says, once she's settled on the blanket over the grass, "what's the craziest rumor you've ever heard about the park?"

I laugh while I'm taking out the sandwiches, salad and fruit. "There was one floating around for a while that the government uses national parks to grow super-potent weed to get kids hooked on it," I tell her. "That one occasionally gets the alt-right prayer groups out here looking for hidden marijuana to report."

"And probably some potheads looking to score some premium product, too," Hannah adds.

"Yeah, that too," I chuckle. I start in on some of the salad I made, and Hannah takes a swig of water before taking a bite of her sandwich.

"I wouldn't think a big tough guy like you would be interested in having a picnic in the woods," she says, raising an eyebrow.

"Hey--I love being in the woods, and I love to eat. What's not to like?" I ask, shaking my head.

Hannah laughs. "Well, what's keeping Yogi Bear and Boo-Boo from coming to steal your picnic basket, Ranger?" she asks with a flirty grin.

I chuckle at that. "Bears aren't usually interested in well-hidden picnic coolers," I tell her. "Generally, if they're going to bother to raid something, it'll be out in the open, like if someone leaves the remains of a campfire feast out."

"Good to know," Hannah says. For a few minutes we eat in silence, but I can see the gears turning in her mind, the way she's looking off into middle-distance, thinking about what she's going to ask me next.

The clan keeps checking in occasionally, but I'm able to keep that in the back of my mind, like I always do. Now that I have a little time to sit here and relax, I can't help but scan my eyes over Hannah's curves. I'd checked her out the night before, of course, but the sunlight does something special to her light brown hair and makes her hazel eyes sparkle. I keep finding myself glancing at the way her tits strain at the fabric of her sweater, or thinking--almost against my will--about how she must taste, what it would be like to feel her thighs close against my head as I devour her.

The grapes I'm eating don't taste half as sweet as I'm sure she would, and as I let my mind wander a bit more, I can feel my dick getting hard--not enough to be embarrassing, but enough to make my pants feel uncomfortably tight; enough to make me sweat a bit.

"So," I say, plucking another cluster of grapes out of a plastic container, "what else do you want to know about the park?"

"I'm really just trying to get to the bottom of what's behind its creation," Hannah says with a shrug. "Like any journalist, if I see something vague that doesn't quite add up, it's like some switch in my brain flips; I have to know what the answers are."

I smile at that, but I can only hope that Hannah isn't as good at her job as her questions lead me to believe.

"There's nothing sketchy going on," I say matter-of-factly. "Davis was a great man, and most of the conservationists--including Rockefeller--were pretty decent, beyond the whole 'super-capitalist' thing they had going on."

Hannah snorts. "But those people seem to have always had shadowy personal lives," she points out. "I mean, just take the Kennedys, for example. There was that Kennedy sister whose dad sent her to get a lobotomy because she was, I guess, mildly mentally ill and disobedient, and she ended up pretty much becoming a zombie. And no one talks about it when they're talking about JFK."

"So, what's your pet theory? What skeletons do you think are lurking in the closets of the people who wanted--shockingly--to save some of this beautiful land from being turned into factories and strip malls?"

Hannah shrugs. "I have no idea," she admits. "Not *yet,* anyway."

"Well, I wish you luck in getting to the bottom of it," I say. "I can't help you tease out these fringe theories; I only know the official story."

"Of course, you do," Hannah says. She grabs a ripe plum out of the cooler and takes a bite. Watching her, seeing the juice dribble down her chin onto the front of her shirt; noticing the look of pure pleasure on her face at the flavor turns me on beyond belief.

I want nothing more than to pin Hannah down on the blanket and taste the plum on her lips, tear her clothes off and make her understand that she belongs to me.

Down, boy! Fuck! I push my primal instinct to the back of my mind and try to get back the control I've prided myself on.

"I'll be happy to show you around a little more," I tell her. "There are some great bird-watching spots around the park, and maybe we'll be lucky enough to get a look at some of the other wildlife from a safe distance."

"I'd like that a lot," Hannah says, nodding her approval.

Before I can suggest that we pack up the remains of our little feast and move on, I hear the unmistakable sound of bears approaching, growling, telling me once again, the politics of my life as a bear are about to collide with my professional life.

CHAPTER FIVE
HANNAH

I see Knox go tense, and my heart starts beating faster. "What's wrong?" He's been a little on edge most of the day, but it's obvious to me that he's alert to something I haven't noticed.

"Bears," he says, hardly above a whisper.

"*Bears?*" I look around; I thought I'd heard something a moment before, but I didn't think anything of it.

"Bears, and they're close," Knox murmurs.

My heart isn't just beating faster in my chest-- it's pounding, my blood is rushing in my ears, and I have no idea what to do with myself.

"What do we do?" Knox rises to his feet in one quick movement; it's almost too fast for me to see, in fact. One moment, he's lounging on the blanket next to me, and in the next, he's heading towards the tree line.

"Stay here," he whispers. "I'll take care of this." I watch him move through the grass in near-silence, and while part of me is pretty sure that of the two of us, he must be the one to know what to do--but another part of me is imagining what would happen next if he gets himself killed by a bunch of bears.

Knox disappears into the woods, and I'm stuck sitting on the blanket with the remainder of the food he brought, wondering what the hell to do if his plan falls apart. I hear movement in the woods and I shiver, thinking of Knox going up against however many bears there are out there.

Aren't bears solitary? They don't wander around in groups, other than, obviously, mother bears with their offspring, right? I couldn't remember ever hearing anything about bears working as a group towards some common goal, but apparently, they did.

After a while, my curiosity got the best of me, and I couldn't resist rising and making my way toward the tree line. I must be out of my mind; it's crazy to think of walking into the woods when there are bears within a short distance of me, but I can't stand not knowing what's going on.

I try to move as quietly as possible through the grass and it occurs to me how strange it was that Knox was able to get into the woods without making a single noise; but then, I remind myself, he's a park ranger; he's used to doing stuff like that.

I slip past the trees and it feels like every inch of my skin is crawling with anticipation. As I step in the direction Knox went in, I start hearing some of what's going on: growls, groans, and the unmistakable sound of foliage being trampled and crunched under enormous feet. I can't hear any sign of Knox, and a terrifying thought occurs to me.

Oh god, what if they got him? What if he's dead?

And then it occurs to me to wonder what the hell I think I'm going to accomplish by going after him, when I don't have any training in dealing with bears *at all*.

I see a blur of dark fur and crouch down, hoping I'm downwind of the huge beasts. I crawl forward, enough to be able to see what's happening, and I'm completely confused: three bears thunder off in the opposite direction of the clearing, muzzles coated in foamy saliva, while two more continue to wrestle. I can't see Knox anywhere, and I lift myself up a bit--still trying to remain hidden--to look for him. Where the hell could he have gone? I thought he was supposed to be taking care of the situation so the bears wouldn't come after us--or more accurately, *me*?

The two bears still fighting are going at it harder than I would have imagined possible, tumbling and growling and even roaring every few moments, and I can't help but just sit there, fascinated and afraid, watching them.

I have no idea what to do. At first, the two bears look almost identical, but as I stare at the fight going on between them, I notice slight differences: one is definitely bigger than the other, even if it's hard to tell from all the movement. One of them has patches of bare skin showing through the fur--maybe from some kind of infection, or mange? I'm not sure. But I definitely feel like the bigger bear is somehow familiar, and somehow comforting. It keeps putting itself between the other bear and the path to where Knox and I had been having our picnic before.

The smaller bear manages to slip past the bigger one, and then looks straight at me. I want to believe that it can't see me, but it's hard to keep that belief up when it licks its chops and starts heading in my direction. Panic washes over me, and before I even know what I'm doing, I get to my feet. My legs prickle with pins and needles from the circulation rushing through them again, and I turn around and begin to run, crashing through the woods.

As I'm heading back in the direction I've come, I spot something: Knox's jacket, on the ground, half-tucked behind a log. That only makes me feel more panicked, reminding me that the one security I have against the bears fighting in the woods is nowhere to be seen. I run past the blanket in the clearing, not even bothering to grab my purse: all I care about is getting away before the bear can catch me.

It isn't until I'm a good half mile down the trail that I realize I don't even know where I am, or where I'm headed. I'm totally lost, and as that realization dawns on me, a sharp, pointed catch lights up along my ribs, and I have to stop running. I slow down and look behind me; the bear either got distracted by the picnic or the other bear caught up to it--whatever the case, it isn't chasing me.

I stop, panting and gasping for breath, and bend forward until my hands are on my knees. My head spins and I feel myself wavering, my knees going rubbery from so much running all at once along with the fear of being chased by at least one bear. I sink down onto my knees and wince at the impact on my hands as I try to catch my breath and--at the same time--figure out what I should do.

"Hannah! Hannah, are you okay?" I scramble up onto my feet just in time to see Knox jogging towards me; his jacket is gone, and there are some scratches across his face and his hands, but otherwise, he looks just fine.

"Where the hell did you go?" I dust my hands off on my jeans and look Knox up and down quickly. It definitely looks like something happened to him, but I can't wrap my head around the fact that he somehow disappeared, and then reappeared, not as harmed as I would have thought for a guy who had a run-in with four bears.

"I lured a few of the bears away, and then the remaining ones were fighting it out," Knox tells me.

"One of them chased after me," I say.

Knox nods. "I had doubled back by then. When I saw it going in your direction, I headed it off and sent it back into the woods, away from the trail," he says.

I look at him for a long moment. Other than his jacket, I'd seen no sign of Knox while I was running from the bear. *He probably took it off and tossed it aside when he started fighting with the bears,* I tell myself, but the whole situation seems so endlessly bizarre.

"Is it safe to go back to the picnic? I left my bag back there," I say.

Knox nods. "I got rid of all of them; they won't be bothering us anymore," he tells me as I look him over. He's obviously been scratched up, but it looks more like the work of being whipped in the face by branches and vines rather than claws. Of course, there's no way for me to know what really happened between the time he left the blanket and when he reappeared on the trail, coming to me; something about the whole situation just doesn't add up.

"I guess I have to thank you again," I say as I start back in what I hope is the right direction.

Knox falls into step next to me. "Oh?"

I grin at him. I don't want him to think I doubt his story, but in the back of my mind, I'm trying to piece together a scenario that would both explain what I saw and validate his story.

"Yeah, you've saved me twice," I point out.

"Just doing my job," Knox says. He moves a little closer to me, and I catch a whiff of some kind of deep, earthy musk clinging to him; it doesn't smell bad exactly, but very--*very*--primal. It must be something from the bears, I decide, putting it out of my mind. But even as we finally get back to the blanket, I find the smell clinging to Knox is actually kind of appealing in a strange way.

"Wow, that must get the adrenaline pumping," I say absently. "Chasing off bears, I mean."

"It definitely makes me feel manlier than--say--having a picnic," Knox admits.

I have to chuckle at that. I glance over at him as I'm gathering up my things from the blanket, and I can't help but notice there's a definite bulge at the front of his jeans. The sight of it makes the blood rush to my face and I look away quickly. Either Knox is turned on by me, or he's turned on by fighting bears; I'm not sure which one is more concerning.

"So...I guess that effectively derailed our interview," I say, reaching into my bag and turning off the recorder.

"We can start back up if you want," Knox suggests.

I shake my head. "Nah...although, if you're free later in the week, I might circle back and get some more quotes from you," I say. Suddenly, everything catches up with me, and I feel like I can't get up from the blanket and move another step. My legs feel like they're weighed down with lead, and my heart's only just started to slow down in my chest. "I think I could happily take a nap right here," I tell Knox wryly.

"Not used to running for your life, I take it," he says with a little grin.

"Not really, no," I admit. I lay back on the blanket while he finishes clearing up the remainder of the food, putting it in the cooler. I take a swig of my water and watch him. *God, he's hot.*

"If you want, I can give you a leg rub," Knox suggests. "Might help."

I raise an eyebrow, but I can't think of an actual reason to say no. "Okay," I say, after thinking it through for a moment.

What could possibly go wrong?

CHAPTER SIX
KNOX

I couldn't resist offering to give Hannah a leg massage. It popped into my mind and the words instinctively rolled off my tongue. I had to touch her.

Do you have the trail for those assholes?

I project the thought out to the rest of my clan, who are scattered around the park. As soon as I'd realized they were in the woods near where Hannah and I sat, I'd sent out a call to let my clan know. Even though three of the four bears had fled, I was fairly certain they'd be tracked down this time. The last bear, Harris, the one I'd been fighting when Hannah had come upon us, was unconscious several yards away, about to be secured by my clan. I'd drawn a considerable amount of blood from each of the outsiders, which is much harder to hide than other scent-marks.

Don't worry, Boss, we're closing in on them, Cassidy projects to me.

I turn my attention back to Hannah. "Why don't I start at your ankles," I suggest.

I can't back down from the offer now--not when she's accepted it.

Hannah looks up at me for a moment, "Really, you don't have to--"

"I insist."

She blushes, but I settle myself at her feet, kneeling there. I pick up one of Hannah's ankles and begin kneading it slowly, working from the Achilles tendon up toward her calf. Hannah moans, and the sound of her--mingled with her irresistible scent--is almost more than I can stand. I try to take shallow breaths, mostly through my mouth, but I can still feel the tension in her body as I switch to her other ankle and then start moving up to massage her calf.

Even through her jeans, I can feel the strength in her legs; the heat of her body. After changing into my animal form to protect her--and get rid of the punks that have no business in this territory--my bear consciousness is still partly in command of me, and hard to push back. The feeling of her body, the smell of her, is driving me crazy.

She should be mine. Except she's not a bear-- she's not *any* kind of shifter. How could I want her? How could she smell like something that belongs to me? Is it possible that a human...could be my *mate*?

She moans again when I get up to just above her knee, and I look up at her face. "You're enjoying yourself," I murmur, smiling a bit at her. Hannah's cheeks flush; she looks away and then quickly back at me, and I can see the rosiness spread across the little slice of her chest that's visible at the neck of her sweater. Breathing in deeply, I can actually *smell* her arousal, rolling off her in waves which makes it impossible to focus on anything but my ever-growing desire for her.

"Maybe we should stop," Hannah says, her voice cracking. "I mean, I don't want to be inappropriate. I don't want there to be any questions about whether my article is objective or not."

I chuckle. "Can't have that, can we?"

I lean in a little closer to her. I can't help it, it's like her body itself is drawing me in, and I can feel her pulse quickening; I can smell the way her arousal is deepening as my thumbs work at the muscles of her thighs, kneading and rolling.

"No one would ever have to know," I say. No one in my clan needs to find out that I want to devour this human female whole; that I want to gorge myself on the honey I can smell between her thighs and feel her body wrapped around me.

"Someone could see us," Hannah whispers.

I laugh again. "Other than the wildlife, not many people are going to head this far away from the trail," I point out. "If you can tell me that you don't *want* me to fuck your brains out right here and now, I'll stop, and I'll even apologize for coming onto you."

I hold her gaze. We both know she can't honestly say she doesn't want it.

"I do," she admits. "I just don't think I should get involved with someone who's a source for my article."

I lean in and brush my lips against hers, letting my fingers stop exploring her thighs and instead move up to cup the full tits I've wanted to get my hands on all day. She murmurs something against my mouth, but it doesn't sound like a protest at all; more like a moan of pleasure.

I deepen the kiss and brush my thumbs against her hardening nipples, straining at the fabric of her bra under her sweater. There's no question she's turned on, and I'm so hard that I ache, my cock throbbing in my jeans.

Hannah presses up against me and the feeling of her body against mine is so perfect--the feral consciousness that controls half my mind roars with pleasure, and all I want is to rip her clothes off and unleash my wild urges without restraint. But the human part of my mind comes to the forefront just in time to remind me Hannah isn't ready for that--

she might never be.

I pin Hannah on the blanket, barely holding myself over her, and probe her mouth with my tongue; I can taste the fruit she ate last, and the lingering sweetness of her own natural flavor, spurring me to taste her elsewhere, waking the hunger that gnaws at my bones. I drop down to her throat, nuzzling her there, inhaling the sweet-musky scent of her pheromones.

"If you want me to stop, say the word and I will, immediately," I tell her as I lick the spot just under her jaw where I can feel her pulse fluttering.

"Don't...stop," she says breathlessly, and no two words have ever been better in the history of language. I start pawing at her clothes, trying to find the hem of her sweater. The only thing in the entire world I want right now is to see her fully naked--and then, after that, I want to eat her until she gushes in my mouth.

Hannah manages to pull my shirt over my head and her hands dance over my back, pausing when she finds the scratches and scrapes from my fight with the other bears. They've already almost healed completely, but hopefully, she won't notice.

I somehow get her sweater off, and then her bra, freeing her gorgeous tits from their prison, and I take a second to just admire them. "God, Hannah," I say, shaking my head at how fucking hot she is, laid on her back, her chest flushed, the pale skin of her breasts ending in two pale pink areolas with nipples as hard as pebbles.

I dip down and grab both of them, bringing first one and then the other up to my mouth. Hannah's skin tastes as good as her lips, with a little salt mingled in from her sweat and the faintest leftover traces of her fear from when she'd been running away from one of the bears earlier. I suck each of her nipples and swirl my tongue around the sensitive little nubs, and the sound of Hannah moaning out, her breath catching in her throat as her body heats up under me, is like a drug. I want to make this woman come harder than she's ever come before in her life.

I spend a little time on her tits and then work my way down along her abdomen, reaching for the fly of her jeans. I can't possibly wait another second; I can't hold myself back. I get her jeans and panties down over her hips and she squirms beneath me, kicking them the rest of the way down her legs.

With her finally naked, I can hold back enough to appreciate the view in front of me: Hannah's tits rise and fall, shaking a bit from how hard and fast her breaths are coming, and as my gaze wanders down over her body, I notice she's got a little tattoo of a heart on the inside curve of her hip. But that's less important than the sight of her pussy, her light brown hair trimmed down to a little patch, her folds wet with her fluids. The scent of her arousal makes my mouth water, and all I can think about is devouring every last bit of her.

I spread her legs wide and dive between them, barely giving Hannah a chance to realize what's happening before I bury my face against her soaking wet folds. I lap up every last bit of her fluids, tasting every inch of her; Hannah's hips buck against me, but my arms have her pinned right where I want her. She tastes every bit as good as I could have imagined, her sweet flavor coating my tongue, dripping down my chin as she gets more and more turned on.

I slow down to take my time with her, teasing her, bringing the tip of my tongue up to the firm little bead of nerves and then back down to her inner folds. I suck as much of her into my mouth as I can, like eating an overripe peach, swallowing and worshipping her, probing her, devouring her while she moans, cries out and writhes underneath me.

I keep her right on the razor's edge, reading her body, bringing her right up to the moment before she could come, and then back off just enough to keep her from reaching her peak. Hannah gets hotter and hotter, her hands grabbing at my head and shoulders, her fingernails digging into my skin, her thighs tightening around me the second, then the third time I bring her to the edge.

All the while, I can feel myself getting more and more turned on, my dick hard as a rock, hot as molten metal, trapped in my pants. I can't wait to feel her wrapped around me; I can tell she's tight, and she's so hot and wet that even before she comes, my face is soaked.

I finally give her what I know she needs, sucking her clit between my lips, swirling my tongue around it as Hannah gasps, shakes and almost screams with pleasure as she comes. Her fluids gush against my chin and I suck as much of her into my mouth as I can, alternating between keeping enough pressure on her clit to keep her climax going and swallowing down her fluids, lapping them up eagerly.

I feel her climax starting to ebb and I gradually slow down, pulling back bit by bit. By the time I'm hovering inches away from Hannah's pussy, she's panting and gasping, trembling all over.

"That...was amazing," Hannah says, opening her eyes and tilting her head just enough to look down at me between her legs. I laugh, planting a wet kiss on her tattoo before making my way up her body to kiss her lips.

"That can't have been the first time someone's gone down on you," I say, rubbing myself against her leg. If I don't get inside of her soon, the animal side of my consciousness is fairly sure I'll die.

"No, but it was definitely the first time someone did it that...enthusiastically," Hannah says.

I laugh again, kissing along the column of her throat and bringing my hands up to her tits to tease her nipples.

"You taste good enough that I could eat you all night," I tell her.

"That could get in the way of getting anything else done, like sleeping," Hannah points out playfully. "And from the hard-on I feel in your pants, you're about to pop; eating me all night wouldn't help you in that department."

"You're right about that, I suppose." I sigh, and then moan as Hannah reaches down to rub me through my pants. The animal part of my brain wants me to roll Hannah over and take her, filling her up hard and fast.

I'm teasing Hannah's nipples all the while, and I can see and feel her starting to get turned on all over again. *Imagine what it would be like if you could mate her. Imagine making her yours and having her waiting for you every night.*

Hannah gasps as I twist one of her nipples a little harder than I intend to, but the half-moan at the back of her throat tells me she likes it, nonetheless. "You seem pretty eager," I tell her.

"Your fault," she says, grinning up at me, "for getting me all hot like this."

Somehow, she's managed to get my fly open without me noticing, and when her hand begins to stroke my cock, I reach the point of no return. I *need* to feel her.

"So, you're really okay with this?" I ask, as soon as I can actually talk.

"I'm definitely okay with it," Hannah says. I lick my lips, still able to taste her, and then pull back, giving into the instincts taking control of my mind.

I turn Hannah over onto her stomach and pull her up by the hips, and she scrambles to get into the position I clearly want her in, holding herself up on her elbows with her ass in the air. The view from behind is every bit as amazing as it is from the front, and I push my jeans down over my hips, my boxers going with them, taking in the sight of Hannah's delicious curves.

I guide the tip of my cock against her and hold onto her hip with one hand, keeping her right where I want her. I thrust into her from behind all at once, too turned on to take my time; Hannah moans out and her body squeezes me, flexing and then relaxing around my aching cock. It feels so goddamn good, I almost lose it right then and there. I have to stay still for a few seconds, breathing to push down the instinct to come right away. After a few moments, I've got control of myself again and start moving inside of her, pulling almost all the way out and thrusting back in, finding my rhythm.

Hannah feels so good--hot, wet and tight around my cock--and from the sounds leaving her throat, she feels the same way about me. I reach around the curve of her hip and find her clit, and begin to stroke it in time to my thrusts.

"Fuck, Hannah!" I lean over her, moving faster as the feeling of her body turns me on more and more, pounding into her from behind. She moans and cries out, pushing her hips back to take me deeper and deeper, falling into my rhythm, her body flexing around me in tight little spasms.

I manage to hold back long enough to bring her to another climax, and then I give up control again, pounding her hard and fast as the tension deep down in my balls hits a fever pitch right before it unravels. It feels so good--so right--to come buried deep inside her, and I let out an involuntary roar, the animal part of me laying claim to the woman under me, as wave after wave of pleasure temporarily blots out everything else that was ever on my mind.

We collapse together on the blanket and I roll over to my side, wrapping my arm around her tightly, pulling her close to my chest. I feel my heart pounding against her back as I nuzzle in her ear and whisper, "I could certainly get used to this."

I really could; I just have to be careful. I have a lot to protect and a lot at stake.

CHAPTER SEVEN
HANNAH

There was something about the combination of running for my life, the way Knox's massage felt, and something I can't quite put my finger on that just threw my inhibitions--and perhaps, better judgement--completely out the window. I can't deny the tenderness between my legs is pretty damn satisfying, but I might have jeopardized my own article by getting too close to a source. It's totally not like me; I've never done anything like this before in my entire life.

Knox just walked me to my car, and I'm getting my gear secured in the passenger seat, ready to go back to Mary's place and start transcribing the interview. *He's hot, and that was definitely the best sex I've ever had--but was it worth fucking up my career?*

"Hey, you!"

I jump as I hear someone tapping on my window, and at first, I feel defensive; I'm expecting the woman standing there to say she saw me and Knox having sex. Her jet-black hair is pulled back into a messy ponytail, and she's dressed in a pair of shorts and a long-sleeved t-shirt that says "Question Authority." *Seems a little chilly for the weather to me. Must be a local*, I assume.

"Can I help you?" I cautiously begin to put my window down, stopping after a few inches.

"You were talking to the administrator, right? Just a little while ago?"

I nod, wondering what that has to do with anything, but at least it seems like this chick doesn't know what he and I were just up to at the other end of the park.

"Yeah, I was interviewing him about an article I'm working on about the history of Acadia and the National Park Service," I tell her. "I'm a journalist with *New World* magazine." The woman looks me up and down quickly and then comes to some kind of decision.

She peeks over her shoulder and then turns back to face me. "This place has secrets, you know," she tells me. "I live around here, and I know it's Knox Bernard's job to keep those secrets under wraps."

I raise an eyebrow at this. "What *kind* of secrets?"

I'm expecting her to say something about Masons, Sons of Columbus, or Pagans, or maybe Knox's favorite crazy theory that the government is growing super-potent pot at the state and national parks.

"Well, this is gonna sound crazy, but he's," she peeks over her shoulder again, then whispers, "some kind of *supernatural creature*."

Okay, well that's not what I would have thought. It sounds even more bizarre than anything else I've heard associated with Acadia, but the woman is telling me this with absolute seriousness.

"Every month, right around the full moon, Acadia issues special alerts to campers, advising them to avoid leaving the trails at night."

"I'm sorry, but that just sounds..." I shrug. I don't even know how to finish that sentence without being rude or potentially offensive.

"The full moon is in two days," the woman points out. "You can find out for yourself. Whatever it is they're doing here, that's the best time to see it with your own eyes."

I cross my arms over my chest and look at the woman for a moment, and ponder what she's telling me. I didn't really believe any of the conspiracy theories I'd read, but if it checks out that this woman is, in fact, a local, and even *she* thinks there's something going on here, it would be worth investigating, wouldn't it? And it's not like it would be outside of the scope of what I'm working on.

"I have to admit, this is one of the strangest things I've ever heard. I don't mean to come across as rude, but why should I believe you?" I look around; people are starting to leave the park as it's beginning to get dark and the air is getting colder. "How do I even know you're a local? You don't have the same accent as everyone else."

"Here, look at my ID," the woman says. "I moved up here about five years ago." She takes a wallet out of her shoulder bag, which is covered with all sorts of anti-establishment pins, and fumbles with it for a moment before handing me a Maine driver's license. This is definitely her picture; the license reads: *Jessica Durand, date of birth August 24, 1980. Female, 5'7"*, and the address is a place in Bar Harbor, not far from Mary's.

"Okay, so you're a local," I concede. "How do I know you're not just putting me up to this because you have something against Mr. Bernard?"

Jessica leans in a bit toward me. "Look, believe it or don't believe it, but I want answers. Something's up, and Knox and his other freaky buddies at the park are trying to keep it quiet." She gives me a hard look. "You're with the press; you could blow this thing wide open."

Before I can ask her another question, Jessica backs off and calls out to someone who's apparently a friend of hers, leaving me all by myself to contemplate the news.

At first, I reject the idea altogether; after all, this sounds like it's just another rumor; there's probably nothing to it. Jessica--whoever she is--might just be someone who's got a crush on Knox; maybe she's just trying to make things difficult for him because she suspects that I'm into him or something.

I look over toward Jessica again, and it seems that whoever she's speaking to doesn't want to take what she's dishing out. The woman's holding her hands up, waving her off and shaking her head as she walks in my general direction. I see Jessica lumber off down the road, seemingly talking to herself.

I decide to hop out of my car and flag down the other woman. "Hey, do you know her?" I ask, pointing in Jessica's direction.

She stops, turning her head my way and rolls her eyes. "God, it's like you can't come here without being trapped in a verbal headlock by that freak."

I cross my arms and lean back against my car, furrowing my brow. "I just met her for the first time. She's got some…strange ideas about this place; that's for sure."

"She's got some strange ideas about *everything*," she replies. "If I were you, I'd steer clear of her. That is, unless hashing out nonsense with an eccentric weirdo for hours is your cup of tea."

"Good call," I say. "Thanks for the heads up."

She waves and continues down the path, heading deeper into the park, and I hop back in my car and turn the ignition, wondering what the hell just happened as the car sputters to life. But even as I drive out of the park, passing Jessica on the way, I feel that little tingle that comes along with a good story; that little itch to figure something out and get to the bottom of it.

Before Knox and I hooked up, I'd definitely noticed that he seemed to stonewall questions about the founding of the park and the people involved in it. That could be nothing--or it could be that Jessica was on to something after all, and that Knox is, in fact, trying to cover something up.

If there *is* something going on during the full moon, what would it hurt to find it out? I could come by the park at night, and see for myself.

CHAPTER EIGHT
KNOX

"We've got three of the four, that should be enough," Trent says to me as we head back to the park offices.

I shake my head; as long as Shawn is out there, everything that Acadia stands for is in danger of being exposed.

"If he gets caught doing something stupid, we're fucked," I point out.

"He's got to be smart enough to not want to draw attention to himself while he's alone," Trent counters.

I shrug. "He and the other three tried to attack *a fucking journalist* the other night," I insist. "None of those pricks seem to have any common sense or regard for Acadia whatsoever."

"They couldn't have known she was a journalist," Trent says.

"They didn't, but they shouldn't be going after *any* humans. Who knows how long they've been putting us all at risk, and for all we know, those dicks could have been shifting right in front of the park visitors." I shake my head and start taking my radio and other gear off as we step into the office together. "They're just sloppy. And lazy."

"Well, we've got the clan looking for him; he can't stay hidden forever," Trent says.

"Tomorrow's the full moon, the first night of it, anyway," I tell him. "I don't want anyone here to be under threat from that asshole."

"I'm less worried about our kind than any human bystanders that might be lurking," Trent says. "We can more or less take care of ourselves."

Because it's neutral territory, every month during the full moon, Acadia plays host to dozens of shifters from the surrounding area. We gather in an incredibly remote section of the park, spacious enough to allow our kind to run, hunt, forage and express our full primal nature--something that most shifters around the country would rarely get to experience otherwise.

My clan has always been known for being a gracious host. As the Alpha, it's my job to make sure that there's nothing tainting Acadia as neutral territory; I can't allow anyone to try and claim it as a domain for their own pack or clan. Shawn, along with his buddies Harris, Kevin, and Jamie, are proving to be a sizeable threat to maintaining our neutrality.

I'm confident that I can convince the shifters' conclave to agree that they have to be expelled from the grounds, at the very least. If they decide their transgressions are severe enough, I might even have clearance to execute them, but I'm not going to count on it. But in order to get their opinion, I need to have all four of these degenerates in custody. They won't hold a tribunal otherwise.

"We need to track Shawn down before tomorrow night," I say. "The members of the conclave will be here for the full moon anyway, and we can get them to decide on a verdict."

Trent nods his agreement with me. "The clan has the park cordoned the best they can. I'm sure we'll find him in time."

I send a mental signal to each of the members of my clan, taking note of their whereabouts, touching each of their minds in turn. It's trickier than just calling out to them, but it's something I've worked out over the years of being an Alpha; it's a skill that comes in handy at moments like this.

Trent's right: as I hone in on each of their minds, I can tell the clan is as close as it can be to having the whole park cordoned off. If Shawn tries to leave, then there's a good chance he'll run into someone, or at least pass close enough to be pursued. For the time being--while I'm on official duty--I can't personally do much more.

I sit down and Trent heads out to make his usual rounds. In the back of my mind, I can't help but think about the nosy reporter, Hannah Grant.

With these outsiders treating Acadia like their own personal criminal hunting grounds, her arrival couldn't have possibly come at a worse time.

But right now, I'm not really thinking about how her presence complicates the situation with Shawn and his clan; I'm thinking about how good it felt to be inside of her, and how much I want to taste her again.

She's made herself scarce for the past couple of days since then, but she's been at the forefront of my mind ever since. I sit back in my desk chair and stare up at the ceiling. *She suspects you're covering something up, something you know but that isn't common knowledge--that much she made clear to you before the two of you hooked up.* That should be a red flag right there; I shouldn't try to pursue Hannah any further, unless I'm willing to risk exposing everything my kind has worked so hard to keep secret, but the bear within has been calling out for her ever since our little tryst in the park. I try to shake off the thought, but then remember that she'd promised to circle back to finish our interview, which she hasn't done yet.

"That's as good of an excuse as any to stop by wherever she's staying," I muse to myself. I should be able to pick up on her scent trail and figure out her location; then I can check on her, see if she's got some more questions for me, and hopefully put any ideas she's had regarding conspiracy theories to rest for good. *Maybe then, we could pick up where we left off the other day.*

I wait until my shift is over and change into some street clothes: a pair of jeans, a t-shirt and a thick flannel, along with what I consider to be my off-duty boots. I get onto my bike and gun the engine, checking to make sure it's in peak shape, and then start heading down the main road out of the park.

I don't know exactly where Hannah's staying, so as I pull off the grounds, I slow down, sampling the air as I head towards Bar Harbor.

After a few minutes, I finally catch a hint of that unmistakable scent and begin to follow its trail. There are several different spots in the park's proximity where I can tell she's been: first a gas station, then a gift shop; I pick it up again at a greasy spoon a little further east up Route 233, heading closer to Bar Harbor.

I finally manage to track the scent to a house in a residential neighborhood downtown and spot Hannah's car parked on the street. This is definitely where she's staying; her mark is stronger along the sidewalk and the grass leading from her car to the front door. I park my bike and walk up to the house.

Almost as soon as I knock, a middle-aged woman answers, looking me up and down with interest. "How can I help you?"

"I'm looking for Hannah Grant. She's staying here, right?"

The woman looks me up and down again--a little doubtfully--and then gives me a polite smile. "She's sitting on the porch out back," she says. "You can go around, or I can get you something to drink if you want to cut through the house."

"I'll go around, thanks," I say with a wave. The woman gives me the vibe that she's going to talk my ear off, given half a chance to, and I've got a lot on my mind. I don't want any distractions.

As I head around back and open the gate to the back yard, I spot Hannah sitting at a little patio table with her feet up on another chair, and a laptop in front of her along with a cup of coffee. She's got headphones on and she's typing away, and I have to admit that she looks every bit as good as she ever has: her hair's down, falling to her shoulders, and she's wearing a sweater dress that hugs her curves perfectly, along with a pair of leggings and some knee-high boots. She looks both adorable and hot all at the same time, and I feel like somehow, I haven't been remembering her right at all; the reality is so much better than my memories.

She looks up as I get a bit closer and jumps, almost dropping her laptop. "Whoa! Where did you come from?" She takes her headphones off, carefully sets her laptop down on the table and sits up in her seat, looking at me more intently.

"I remembered you'd wanted to get around to interviewing me again, and I figured now would be as good a time as any," I say.

"Oh! Right. I wrote that down, but I've been diving deeper down the rabbit hole, so to speak, and spaced out on following up with you," Hannah says. "Wait, how did you know I was here?"

I think fast; I couldn't exactly tell her I followed her scent. "Oh, I was just passing through town and I recognized your car on the street, so I decided to stop by and see if you had a little free time to finish things up."

She looks away from me for a second and starts playing with her hands, then smiles at me. *She's hiding something.* "Well, I'm free right now if you are," she says.

"Cool. If you want, I can take you to my favorite bar in town."

"Now that you mention it," Hannah says, shifting a bit in her seat, "I'm technically supposed to be on vacation. I'd love to."

"You are? Then why are you working on an article?" I sit down across from her, and Hannah takes a sip of her coffee.

"They made me take vacation time or I'd lose it," Hannah says. "And I thought that getting out of town for a few days to work on this in a leisurely fashion would be as good as an actual vacation."

I shake my head in disbelief, but admittedly, I'm almost as bad when it comes to vacations; when I take time off, I usually visit other parks, and it isn't as though I'm just visiting as a tourist.

"You need to learn to *actually* take some time off," I tell her. I find myself grinning almost before I realize it, and then I add, "maybe I can help you with that."

"I didn't think you were interested in seconds," Hannah says, and I get a little flash of pleasure at the sight of color lighting up her cheeks.

"Oh, I'm definitely interested; I just figured you wouldn't be in town all that long," I say.

"I was planning on being here a little over a week," Hannah says. "I figured, for the piece I wanted to write, that would be a long enough stay."

"So, there's another, what, five days before you go back?"

I'm torn between feeling relieved and disappointed. On one hand, it's a good thing. I can clear up any misconceptions she might have about the park and she'll finally be out of my hair. But on the other hand, the bear within keeps telling me that Hannah should belong to me and only me. I need her in my cabin, where I can claim her as my mate; where she can bear my cubs for years to come.

I shake the thought from my mind, focusing on the most dire task at hand: protecting the secrets of Acadia. "Alright, then, let's go to the bar and grab a drink, and you can pick my brain a bit more," I suggest.

Hannah nods and stands up, looking around her. "Give me a couple of minutes to put on my jacket, grab my purse and put my stuff away, and I'm game," she says.

"Do you want to ride with me?" I lift my helmet and raise an eyebrow. "I've got a spare helmet."

"Sounds like fun," Hannah says, and once again I see that high, hot color in her cheeks. It's obvious that she's still attracted to me, even if there's something else going on that she's trying to keep to herself.

Maybe after a drink or two, I can get it out of her.

CHAPTER NINE
HANNAH

    Knox's favorite bar is somehow both exactly what I would have expected and nothing like I would have thought it would be.

    I make mental notes for my article: it's obviously been around for a long time, evidenced by its ancient-looking exposed chestnut beams, not to mention, the dated furniture scattered around the place. The guy behind the bar is an elderly man, wearing an old-fashioned dress shirt and vest combination, and I almost want to ask if he pictures himself as being some character in an old-school

Western.

There are a handful of booths along one wall, which is decorated with driftwood, fishing nets and old lanterns, and Knox steers me in that direction. As we sit, I notice the benches are upholstered with an old, but well-maintained fabric, and the table is made of heavy, solid mahogany.

I notice, too, that there's only one TV in the entire bar, off in the opposite corner, away from where we're sitting. There are maybe five patrons watching it, not looking particularly interested as they slowly nurse the beers in front of them.

"So, what else did you want to ask me?"

That's a good question, and I've been trying to figure out what I can do to cover for dropping the ball on that part of my investigation. The ride on the back of Knox's bike was thrilling--enough so that any practical thoughts that had been in my head even seconds before the engine got started just vanished.

"I've been doing some more research, talking to a few locals and some frequent visitors," I explain. "I'm still just trying to piece together whatever I can to explain what doesn't seem clear--in general--about the history of the park and some of the...*events* going on there right now."

"How far have you gotten?" Knox's voice sounds casual, but I pick up on a weird tension underneath.

"I've eliminated a lot of dead ends," I say cheerfully, giving him a wry smile. A waiter comes to the table and Knox orders an Imperial IPA; apparently, the brewery is local.

"And what would you like, ma'am?" I realize I haven't even given any real thought to what I'm going to drink.

"I guess...a Jack and Coke?" It seems like a safe enough drink, as long as I don't have more than maybe one or two. The waiter nods and leaves.

"So, you were saying you've run into a lot of dead ends," Knox says, once we're alone again.

"Yeah," I admit. "I still haven't been able to find the birth certificates for some of the founders, and haven't come up with anything to explain a few of the other gaps. It's actually kind of troubling."

I'm not about to tell him I'm planning on being

in the park tomorrow night to spy on whatever freak show might possibly be going on there.

"And you've been interviewing some of the locals? Anything interesting come up there?"

I shrug off Knox's question. In reality, I've been talking to as many people as possible, trying to do everything I can to either confirm or deny what Jessica told me. But if Knox *is* involved in some kind of a cover-up, I can't tell him anything--not yet, anyway.

"There are a lot of people who really love the park, but they don't know much about its history," I say wryly.

The waiter brings us our drinks and I try to think of a way to get more information out of Knox without revealing the angle of my investigation. We raise our glasses to each other in a wordless toast and I rack my brain for how to phrase my next question.

"It must be really disappointing to have come all this way, only to meet so many dead ends," Knox says.

"It's not too unusual," I tell him. "You win some, you lose some."

"You don't strike me as the kind of woman who accepts losing without a fight," Knox says. "I was actually wondering if you were avoiding me because...well, you know."

"Because we got down and dirty in the woods?" I shake my head. "I mean, that was probably the least professional choice I've ever made, but the real reason is I've been trying to track down as many leads as possible."

"You sound more like a detective than a reporter," Knox suggests.

I laugh. "The two things aren't all that different."

I have to admit, I really like Knox. I feel so comfortable around him, even though my mind is spinning with the notion that he could be involved in some weird secret society.

"That must explain why there's so much crossover," Knox says.

I take another sip of my drink. "So, I've been thinking I might want to wander the park again a bit."

"Well, you'll be happy to hear that we've rounded up all but one of the guys who tried to attack you the other day," Knox tells me.

"Oh! I've been so busy that I totally forgot about it." It's a lie; I've thought about the incident at least once a day since it happened, but I've been working hard not to let it overshadow my investigation.

"The last one's still loose in the park, but the rangers will easily be able to track him down," Knox says.

"So, I'm guessing that you'd want me to be on my guard if I'm in the park on my own," I suggest.

"I'd be happy to chaperone you, if you want, or I can get one of the other rangers to accompany you."

"I don't think that'll be necessary," I say quickly. "It's not all that dangerous; I mean, he's probably trying to avoid anyone's attention, right?"

"True, but I would hate for you to run into him," Knox insists.

"I'll let you know," I say. "In the meantime, what can you tell me about some of the odd layout discrepancies in the park?" That, I hope, should keep his mind occupied for a while.

"Layout discrepancies?" Knox frowns in confusion and takes a sip of his beer.

"There are some spots on maps dated before the opening of the park that have never appeared on any official park maps. It's as if the locations have been intentionally omitted," I say. It's as close as I can come to admitting that I've actually found some information suggesting that something's amiss.

"Well, a lot of those old maps probably aren't all that accurate," Knox says with a shrug.

"These were created by surveyors who were contracted by the government," I point out. "I would hope they'd be accurate."

"If you want to come back to the park with me after this, I can show you some of the documentation we have in the office," Knox says. "I'd be happy to show you the most recent surveys we have on file."

"I'd really appreciate that," I say.

We change the subject for a while and I find out that Knox has worked his way up the hierarchy at Acadia the old-fashioned way, getting his degree and then following it up with conferences and certifications. I have to admit: I had no idea how much work it took to become a national park ranger.

Knox offers to pay for our drinks. He's had two beers and I've had two Jack and Cokes; not enough to get drunk, but enough that there's a bit of a buzz going on in my head, relaxing me a little more. I point out that I can just expense the charge once I get back home, but he insists and settles the bill.

Then I'm on the back of his bike again, and he's driving us to the park, where he has permanent quarters. The vibration of the motorcycle between my legs, along with the fuzziness and warmth of the alcohol in my system, has a predictable effect: instead of being scared that I'm going to fall off the iron horse, or that Knox is going to get hit, I can feel my nerves starting to tingle. I'm only too aware of the feeling of Knox's back pressed against my chest as we make our way out of Bar Harbor.

It's too easy for me to remember how good the sex was, even if having it was a total mistake. The vibration between my legs is almost right up against my crotch, and it's easy for me to see why girls are so into riding motorcycles with good-looking men. It's like having a relatively low-speed massager up against me; it's not enough to make me climax on its own, but definitely enough to get me hot all over and make me wish I could abandon professional scruples to suggest that he pull over and take me back into the woods and have me again. Especially paired with Knox's warm, muscular body and the musky scent of his cologne.

We park outside of his cabin, and as I get off the bike, I attempt to compose myself. *What the hell is wrong with me?* I've been attracted to plenty of guys before, but the intense way my body responds to Knox is unlike anything I've ever experienced.

"Something wrong?"

I shake my head and follow Knox's lead as he heads toward the park's office, not too far from his cabin. As we enter, he tells one of the other park employees that he's going to show me some of the surveys and elevation reports. The ranger shrugs and tells me he hopes I have a good afternoon, and then he's gone. And Knox and I are all alone.

Suddenly, I feel like this was a terrible idea, but in spite of that thought, I can't deny that there's still a damp warmth between my legs, and that I'm replaying--in my mind--how good it felt to have Knox deep inside of me. Over the past couple of days since we hooked up, I've had to get myself off with my fingers a few times, remembering our little tryst in vivid detail.

"Okay," Knox says, unlocking a cabinet. "I think I've got the latest ones here; these are official documents. You can even see the surveyors' notes about where they went and how they made their determinations."

"Do you think I could get copies of these? Or maybe take pictures?" Knox takes a thick folder out and sets it down on his spartan desk.

"Sure, if you'd like. I'll have to fill out a form for your request, but there's no reason why you can't include it in the documentation for your article," he says, sounding oh-so-helpful.

I sit down and start looking through the paperwork; it looks, right off the bat, like everything is above-board and meticulously documented.

After a few moments, I sit back, and see Knox watching me intently. "Any particular reason you're staring at me?" I feel the blood rush into my cheeks and I reach up to smooth my hair against my scalp nervously.

"I found the form you need, but I was waiting until you decided to take a break," Knox says. "And then I noticed how cute you look sitting at my desk."

In spite of the focus I've had on the paperwork in front of me, the humming, simmering arousal that I worked up on the motorcycle never quite went away. I sit back a bit from the desk and look Knox up and down. He's just as hot as ever in his street clothes, and I can't help but think how satisfying it would be to tear them right off him.

"Thanks," I say, blushing even harder. I don't know what to do with my hands, my mouth or any part of my body; I'm tingling all over, hot and cold flashes of sensation dancing through my nerves, and I've almost completely forgotten about the survey reports. "I guess I should go ahead and fill that paperwork out," I say, looking down at the desk.

Knox sets the sheet of paper down on the desk, but instead of stepping away from me, he lingers, and I think--though I can't be sure--I hear and feel him sniff the top of my head. *Did he really just do that?*

I begin filling out the paperwork and Knox leans over me, watching my hand move, and touches my shoulder. Just that little bit of contact is enough to make it even harder to focus, enough to turn me on even more.

Fuck it. You've already rung the bell; there's no reason not to ring it again. I look up at Knox, turning to face him. "Maybe you could show me that cabin they set up for you," I suggest.

Knox smiles slowly. "The office is closed," he points out. "I could lock that door, and no one would come in here. No one would know what's going on."

I feel a little jolt of heat at that suggestion, and I notice the wetness between my legs again, hotter than ever. The idea of having a little fun with the park administrator in his office is just too tempting.

"Go lock it, then," I suggest, my heart beating faster in my chest at the thought.

I watch as Knox crosses the room almost faster than I could imagine possible, and in near silence. He locks the door and then, just as quickly, he's back at the desk, lifting me out of his chair and tilting my chin up to kiss me on the lips.

I reach up and wrap my arms around his broad shoulders, pressing myself against his body; up close to him like this, kissing him back eagerly, it's even easier for me to remember how good our first time together was.

Knox's hands move over my body, touching, caressing and teasing me, and I moan against his lips, gripping him tighter as I get more and more turned on. He cups my breasts in his palms, giving them a careful squeeze, and I shudder, catching his bottom lip between my teeth and nibbling at it playfully.

Then, all at once, we're both pawing at each other's clothes; I fumble a bit with Knox's shirt before I can get it off, but I'm finally rewarded by the sight of his chest. I slowly slide my fingertips over its firm planes and valleys, downward to the fly of his jeans, and my mouth is positively watering, knowing what's inside.

Then Knox lifts me up onto the desk and ducks down, his lips capturing my right nipple. He sucks and licks me, moving from one breast to the other, worshipping me with his mouth; I temporarily forget about the erection I know is standing at attention for me, too wrapped up in the sensations coursing through me to think.

Knox works my breasts with his mouth for what seems like ages, sucking hard enough to make me gasp as his tongue swirls around the hardened nubs. His tongue feels strange; I noticed it the first time we hooked up, but I notice it even more now, how rough it feels against my skin, but it's thrilling all at the same time, sending little jolts of sensation coursing through my body.

Knox reaches down and hooks his fingers under the waistband of my panties, tugging them downward. I push my butt up off the desk to help him, and then, all at once, I'm naked. My hands wander until I find the fly of his pants, and once I manage to figure out where the button and zipper are, I'm somehow getting them open, reaching inside and finding--to my surprise--that he's wearing nothing at all underneath. His hot, rock-hard cock twitches in my hand as I stroke him, and when I get back up to the tip of his erection, I feel the slickness of his precum coating my fingers.

Knox breaks away from my breasts and looks down at me, flushed and panting slightly, a faint, almost-growling sound in his throat, and he looks like a starved animal as he begins to plant his face between my legs.

"As much as I love the idea of you going down on me for hours, I don't think that's necessarily a good idea right here," I say breathlessly.

Knox laughs. "I take your point," he says, kissing me quickly on the lips as I reach for his shaft again. His hand slips up between my legs and he starts stroking me, swirling his fingertips around my clit, falling into the same rhythm I'm using on him until I moan. "God, you're already so wet… and you smell so good…"

"Can we get to the main event?"

I'm so turned on it almost hurts, but at the same time, I don't entirely trust Knox's promise that no one would come barging into his office at any moment. Even though he locked the door, I feel like there's a good possibility that someone could come looking for him or hear us through the wall, but somehow, that makes the whole situation even hotter, even though it makes me worry.

"God, yes," he groans, shoving his pants down to the floor and pushing my hand away from his cock, guiding himself up against me as I squirm to get into the best position, perched on his desk. I love the way the tip of his cock feels against me, and my hips move almost as if they've got a mind of their own, trying to take him inside of me all at once.

Knox thrusts into me and I grab his hips, pulling him closer to take him in as deeply as I can. I reach up for Knox's shoulders, hooking my hands behind his neck, and we start moving together. It feels every bit as good as it did the first time; absolutely perfect, in fact. The heat and hardness of Knox's cock fills me completely and the pacing of his thrusts is exactly what I've been craving. It's almost magical, the way we fit together, and I love it more and more by the moment.

I kiss his lips, his neck, along his shoulders and down onto his chest, licking and nibbling at him playfully, and I hear that somewhat strange low growl again as I feel Knox's body tense up the closer he gets to his peak.

He reaches down and begins stroking and rubbing me as we move together, sending little crackling jolts of pleasure through my body. I cry out and try to muffle it against his shoulder, so wrapped up in the pleasure tingling through my nerves that I can't even think about where we are anymore.

Knox guides me down onto my back and begins slamming into me, hard and fast, looking down at me intently, and I'm helpless in the trap of how good it feels. He unwraps my legs from around his hips and grabs me by the ankles, lifting them onto his shoulders; the shift in position is almost more than I can take, feeling the thickness of him rubbing along my inner walls, pushing deeper than ever inside of me.

I twist my hips to meet his thrusts, trying to hold back, but Knox starts rubbing my clit as he pounds into me and I can't stop myself anymore. I bring my hand up to cover my mouth as the tension deep down between my hips gives away with a snap, and pleasure floods through me. Spasms of sensation ripple through my body and I give into it, writhing on the top of Knox's desk, not caring if I knock anything over or if someone hears me.

I'm so wrapped up in my own pleasure that I barely feel the twitching of Knox's cock inside of me or the way his body tenses. He reaches his climax in the middle of mine, and I'm only just starting to come down when I feel the hot gush of his seed deep inside me. I hear him let out a short, guttural roar as he pounds into me a with few more hard, fast thrusts, almost hitting my cervix, bringing my orgasm back with all new force. Even after Knox finishes, he keeps rubbing my pleasure center, milking my second climax for all it's worth, until I'm limp on his desk, panting and gasping for breath.

"That was even better than the first time," I say as soon as I'm able to talk again.

"It was," Knox agrees. I open my eyes; my head's almost tilted off the desk, and I can still feel him inside of me. I want more, but I know it's a bad idea.

"I should probably get back to Mary's," I say reluctantly.

"Why? I can give you a ride home later," Knox says. I feel him hardening inside of me once more and he starts moving slowly, rocking his hips against mine. "Besides, you're on vacation. You don't have a deadline."

I want to say no--I want to do the right thing, the professional thing--but I have to admit that the idea of round two is *more* than a little appealing...

CHAPTER TEN
KNOX

I want to believe that I can just have my fun with Hannah and then say goodbye to her when she has to return home, but the animal instinct dominating my brain demands that I convince her to stay--that I need to make her mine; make her understand she should be mine--now, more strongly than ever.

"Hey, you hungry?"

Hannah perks at that suggestion and I feel like a champ for coming up with a good, valid reason to keep her around me for a little while longer.

"I could eat," she says. "But don't I kind of owe it to you to take care of dinner? You made lunch for us the other day and paid for our drinks."

"If being square bothers you so much, why don't you just help me cook something back at my place?" I ask. For a second, it looks like Hannah is going to try and argue the point further, but she shrugs it off.

"I guess that'll work," she says, smiling wryly.

"We'll eat and then I'll take you back to your place," I suggest. *And then I'll convince you to stay the night.*

As we walk from the office over to my cabin, I try to remember whether it's clean enough to be seen when I feel Cassidy's mind reaching out to me. It's the worst timing I can imagine, but as the Alpha, it's something I have to deal with.

Knox! Someone let the other three out!

I get a vivid mental picture of the place where members of my clan have been holding Jamie, Harris and Kevin, the guys who had been working with Shawn, and it's empty. I bite back a groan; I have to assume it was either Shawn or someone else working with him, and that somehow, they made it past the two members of my clan who'd been watching over the assholes until we could have the conclave decide their fate.

I have to figure out what to do; I can't just take off and leave Hannah at my cabin without telling her what's going on, or at least giving her a valid excuse.

Call my cell; I'm with a human right now and I need to excuse myself without making her suspicious. Cassidy agrees to my request, and a moment later, my phone rings.

"I should get this," I tell Hannah. She nods and I tap 'accept' and bring the phone to my ear. "What's going on?"

"Are you with that journalist again?"

Cassidy knew about my fling with Hannah because Hannah's scent was still clinging to me when Cassidy and I quartered the woods after Shawn and his crew came after me.

"Yeah," I say, keeping my voice neutral.

"Fun time's over. Tell her, I dunno, that there was another sighting of those bears you dealt with the other day. It's the truth."

I have to admit she has a point. I acknowledge and end the call, and turn to Hannah.

"I need to step out for a bit," I say. "Those bears that almost crashed our picnic the other day got out of the observation area, so I need to head out and see what's going on right now."

"If you want," Hannah suggests, as I switch into my work boots, "I could do the cooking while you're out. That would even things out between us, anyway."

"Sounds good," I say with a grin. At least if she's making dinner, I can count on her being occupied enough not to try and snoop. I give her a quick kiss on impulse and then I'm out the door, headed for the scene of the problem.

I try not to think about Hannah, back in my cabin, as I'm walking towards the holding area where Jamie, Harris and Kevin escaped from. The rest of the clan is operating according to an automatic system we put in place for situations like this; the best trackers in the group are already combing through the woods, following whatever scent trail the bears might have left behind, trying to locate them.

"What do we know?"

Trent's waiting for me at the site, and he's looking like his usual, irritable self. "We think that Shawn busted them out somehow," Trent says.

"How did he get past security? How did they, for that matter?"

That's the biggest issue: there should have been someone watching to make sure the guys we already had in custody didn't break out.

"Matilda and Harold were on duty, and they're nowhere to be found," Trent says. "We don't know if someone took them out, or if they were helping with the breakout, for whatever reason."

Matilda and Harold are a much older than me, ages 70 and 75, respectively, and they'd been living in the area much longer than I have. They've always been pretty rank-and-file; I've had no problems with them betraying my trust, but there's always the possibility that Shawn or one of the others found a way to tempt them.

"So, we have some people looking for Shawn and his crew, and others looking for Matilda and Harold?"

I cross my arms over my chest and sample the air with my nose. Even in my human form, my nose is keen, but it would be better if I shifted into the bear that makes up the other half of my identity.

"Yeah, I've been running the coordination from here until you arrived," Trent says, nodding.

I reach out to the rest of my clan, projecting my thoughts as loudly as possible. *Report back every ten minutes. If I have to, I'll call in some Feds, but I'd rather not get them involved.*

Nobody, least of all me, wants to get the FBI involved, but if it means we'll have better chance of capturing these assholes, that might be our best bet. I have to do whatever I can to keep things quiet, and the sheer risk that the four rogue bears bring about to all of us can't be ignored. We can't have them running loose tomorrow night; I've seen firsthand how reckless they are, and there's too great of a risk that they'll stir up a shitstorm with the other shifters that will be here for the full moon.

Even though I have complete confidence in my clan, being the Alpha, I have to be at the forefront of the efforts, so I start to head out in search of the bastards.

Found Shawn! The mental voice of Alex suddenly cuts out as quickly as it popped into my brain, and I feel my adrenaline starting to rise. Obviously, Alex is going to have to fight Shawn to bring him in. With any luck, his fellow instigators will be close by, and we can have the whole situation wrapped up in a matter of an hour or so.

I feel Alex's mind again a few minutes later, and I can sense he's been hurt. He's definitely been in a fight, but I can sense his victorious surge as well, so hopefully, he'll be bringing Shawn in right away. Got him down for the count. Cass is coming to help me bring him in. The son of a bitch knocked me around pretty good.

The reports I'm receiving from the others aren't as promising, and after about an hour of searching--with Shawn unconscious, cooling his heels in the containment shed--I have to go back, or

Hannah will suspect something's gone wrong and might come looking for me. There's no way I'll have her roaming around out here with those jackasses on the loose.

I mentally project a message to my clan, all twenty of them: Everyone keep me posted; I have to run interference with a human. If anything changes, I'll be on the scene within five minutes. Everyone agrees to that and I start to head back to my cabin.

It bugs the hell out of me to hear that no one knows what happened to Matilda and Harold. Are they on my side and injured badly enough that their minds can't respond? Or, for some reason, have they defected and that's why they can't be found anywhere?

I reach out to Trent just as I get to my cabin: Have one of the younger ones check Matilda's and Harold's houses. Trent tells me that he's on it, and I clear out the issue from my mind, keeping one little thread of my thoughts open for someone to get to me. Now isn't the time to have mental shields up.

I decide that I'm going to have dinner with Hannah and then immediately take her home. No matter how much I want to have her again tonight--in my own bed, at that--I have to get her back to her place. This goes beyond the fucking article at this point; she needs to be out of harm's way, and I need to be able to focus on the park and what my clan needs from me.

I have to make phone calls to the members of the conclave, asking them to get here early tomorrow so they can decide how to handle these idiots trying to muck up our neutral territory. I kick the mud off my shoes and make a quick mental list of who I'm going to need to call; the list isn't all that extensive, but it's going to be like pulling teeth to get them all to agree on a final verdict.

I open the door to my cabin and the scent of Hannah's cooking is enough to make my mouth instantly water. Quick sniffs tell me she's made rainbow trout--my favorite--with a lemon butter sauce, roasted broccoli and rice pilaf, and as I inhale again, I pick up on something sweet for dessert; for just a second, the animal and human parts of my consciousness both agree that I need to convince her to stick around. Anyone who can whip up a meal that smells this good in a short time frame, who's also as good in bed as Hannah is, needs to be mine--and it's about damn time that she knows it. I take a deep breath and push that thought completely out of my mind for the time being; I need to focus.

CHAPTER ELEVEN
HANNAH

The whole time we're eating, Knox seems distracted, but every time I mention it, he just says he's thinking ahead to what he has to do the next day around the park.

"Because of that incident with the bears, there's some complicated paperwork I have to fill out."

"You were able to catch them and get them contained again?"

Knox shakes his head. "We got one of them; I've got trackers out after the others, so I decided to come back here and have a solid meal," he says, smiling at me in that charming way he has. "Besides, I wouldn't want all your hard work to go to waste."

"And then you're going to drop me off back at Mary's, right?"

I don't think that's actually what I want, though. There's a very strong part of me that's begging for Knox to invite me to stay, wrapped in his muscular arms all night, but the rational side of me knows I need to be working on my article. More importantly, I need to look over the maps and survey reports to figure out the right places to check out tomorrow night.

"If that's what you want, then I'm happy to take you home," Knox says, and based on the tone of his voice, it seems like that's exactly what he wants to do. *That's weird. I could have sworn--right when he walked in, at least--that he definitely wanted me to stay.* But I push the weirdness of the situation out of my mind. I should be relieved that he wants to take me home; I should be planning to expose him, after all. *This is why journalists aren't supposed to get too close to their subjects. Or sources. Or whatever Knox is.*

"Yeah, that's probably the best idea," I admit, even though it pains me a little bit.

Why am I getting so attached to this guy? It can't just be the great sex, though that's a *major* point in his favor; it's not like I haven't ever had good sex before. And we haven't interacted enough to justify me having any kind of emotional connection with him, although I have to admit, having him rescue me from a potential attack and chasing off those bears probably accelerated things, from an attachment standpoint.

We finish eating and I start to gather up the plates. "I whipped up a couple of chocolate lava cakes while I was waiting," I say, blushing a bit. "Do you like chocolate?"

"Who doesn't," Knox laughed.

"I figured it would be a good way to use my time that wouldn't include snooping around your house."

"Well, I appreciate you not snooping," he says, sitting back from the little table.

After he'd left, I had actually gotten a chance to appreciate the place; it's cozy, comfortable and clean, which I'm not sure if I should have expected or not. He's got an overstuffed, distressed leather couch in the living room, and when I peeked into the bedroom, I saw a plush, sprawling bed that I bet I'd sleep really well in--especially after another tumble between the sheets with him.

But I know better. I'm only here for a few more days, and I'm better off keeping my mind off any opportunity to have sex with Knox again, no matter how satisfying it would be.

I grab a butter knife and slide it around the edges of the two lava cake ramekins, putting a plate on top of them so I can flip them over and portion them out onto two dessert plates. I grab a tub of vanilla ice cream from the freezer, and after dropping a generous scoop next to each little cake, I place the plates down on the table. I watch Knox drag a spoon through his cake, allowing the liquified chocolate to ooze from its center. He eats it with gusto, and I feel a kind of pride I haven't felt in ages: the pride that comes along with seeing someone you have feelings for enjoying something you made. It's been a couple of years since I cooked for anyone; I'd almost forgotten how much I enjoy it.

"So, what's your schedule like for the next few days? If it's okay with you, I might need to ask you a few more questions." In truth, I need to know when he'll be occupied so I can sneak off to the park during the full moon to complete my investigation.

"Well, I'm going to be really busy for the next two days. Lots of paperwork, on top of a seasonal check of different sites around the park to make sure the wildlife populations are doing what they should." He gives me a little grin. "This cake is amazing, by the way."

"Just something I learned from my mom," I tell him, shrugging off the compliment. Although it feels really good, I need to stop opening myself up to opportunities for Knox to praise me, if I'm going to maintain any kind of objectivity.

"Please thank her for me," Knox says.

I laugh, "I will. So, I guess maybe I'll meet up with you again in three days?"

If I can get a little more detail out of him, I can make sure that I'm not going to end up running into him on the park grounds.

Then, too, I remind myself that the full moon is going to be over the next two days; that's pretty telling that Knox is going to be super busy. *He gave you a perfectly rational reason for that,* I tell myself, but at the same time, I can't help but hope that I'll find something out. By now, I'm convinced that there's *something* to uncover.

"I'd be happy to meet up with you for lunch in three days," Knox says. "I can cook something for you…to even the score."

I roll my eyes. "I used *your* groceries; I'm pretty sure we're even," I say. "There's no need for you to one-up me."

"I'm kind of a traditionalist, I guess," Knox says. "I like to provide for someone I'm sleeping with."

"We're not sleeping together," I point out. "We've had sex a couple of times, but we haven't actually slept in the same bed."

Knox laughs. "If you want to spend the night, then, I'll be free that evening," he suggests with a little grin.

I'm about to respond to that when a troubled look comes over his face for just a second; it's gone before I can even fully see it, but the brief little flicker is enough to derail my train of thought.

"Yeah, maybe we'll see if we'd be compatible bed mates. Do you hog the covers?" I ask.

I know I shouldn't have said that. The last thing I need to do is encourage this kind of banter, but I can't help myself. There's just something about Knox that overrides all my sense of professionalism.

"I don't think you'll have to worry about being cold when you're in *my* bed," Knox says.

I shake my head, rolling my eyes as I blush. "We'll see about that; I might still be focused on getting the last details of the article together by then," I say.

"It still seems like kind of an odd way to spend a vacation," Knox tells me. "When are you going to learn how to relax?"

"*Relaxing* didn't get me where I am today. Besides," I counter, "I'd say I've been relaxing plenty." In fact, in a certain light, I'm probably relaxing far too much.

Our cakes are gone and I can't think of any real reason to maneuver Knox into letting me stay; he insists that he'll do the dishes when he comes back from dropping me off, and that *he* has to be the one to take care of them, because I did the cooking. It's actually a refreshing attitude.

"Do you want to borrow a jacket? It's gotten colder since we rode out here," Knox says.

I accept his offer and he drapes one of his jackets around me. It smells like him--deeply--and I get a little thrill of pleasure at the scent and the warmth of it. It's so nice, and for a few seconds, as I get onto the bike behind Knox, I really wish I could spend more time with him. And maybe just not tonight. I want to forget about my article altogether and just ride out our passions until we both fall asleep.

But throughout the entire ride back to Mary's place, I'm busy pushing my mind to focus on the real reason I'm in Bar Harbor. It isn't for the leaves, it isn't for the beauty of the park, and it isn't to fool around with tough, good-looking park rangers. It's to get a good story about Acadia and the National Park Service.

The vibration between my legs is distracting, but I manage to keep my mind where it is, and before I know it, Knox is coming to a stop outside of Mary's place, turning off the engine to his bike and putting down the kickstand. I feel almost disappointed; in the back of my mind, I've kind of been hoping that he would turn around at some point. But he didn't, and if I have to get down to work, then so does he, and it's for the best that we both stay on our own pages.

But when he walks me up Mary's front steps, both of us have a crisis of resolve. "Why don't you hold onto the jacket until we meet up again? It looks nice on you," Knox says, as we step up to the door.

"I appreciate it; it's really warm."

It sounds terrible, but I have no idea what to say--or even what I *should* say--to the man who I'm becoming so attached to, but obviously won't have any contact with after the next few days.

Before I can come up with something a little more compelling, Knox leans in and brushes his lips against mine, and any thought I have about how much better it is for me to make sure I get my work done dissolves instantly. I instinctively wrap my arms around his neck and press against him, hoping that he'll pick me up and carry me back to his bike, telling me he's taking me to his place.

We stand like that for what seems like ages, and Knox deepens the kiss, plunging his tongue past my lips, tasting me and letting me taste him. It feels so good, and I can't deny that I feel like I belong in his arms, that his lips feel perfect against mine and I want nothing more in the entire world than to just keep going.

But I make myself do the responsible thing. I pull back just as Knox's hands are slipping up under my hem to get at the bare skin underneath and shake my head. "We both have a lot of work to do," I say shakily.

"You're right," Knox says, but I can hear he doesn't want to say it any more than I want him to. Neither of us wants to break apart, but we both know we have to; I can feel it in the way he holds my body against his just a little bit tighter for another second before letting me go. "I'll see you in a couple of days, and we can see about whether we're both free to spend the night, okay?"

I nod, too breathless and too turned on to trust myself to make the right response if I try to speak. Knox grins as if he knows exactly what's on my mind, and reluctantly steps back.

"Good night," I manage to say, and then I force myself to turn around and get my key in the lock. The first night that I got here, Mary told me that she locks up as soon as it's dark, even though her neighborhood isn't dangerous, just as a matter of practice.

"Good night," Knox calls to me from across the yard.

I force myself to open the door, walk through it, and close it behind me. I take a deep breath and decide that before I get down to work, I'll take a shower.

CHAPTER TWELVE
KNOX

I look around and try to push the restless, anxious feeling from my mind, but it's impossible to. It's only minutes before the moon will rise, and my clan only managed to capture the last of the escaped bears an hour ago. During the search, we'd all been devastated to pick up on a signal from Trent, alerting us that he'd found the remains of Matilda and Harold in the underbrush near the tail end of Richardson Brook: *They were attacked, and they've got Shawn's mark all over them. I can tell they didn't go down without a good fight, though.*

How fucking pathetic is Shawn, anyway? Going after a couple of elderly bears? My blood begins to boil, but I force myself to pause and take a deep breath. *Justice will come soon enough*, I remind myself. Waiting for the members of the conclave to arrive--now, more than ever--is like waiting for the axe to fall.

The rest of my clan has already started assembling in our usual meeting spot in the park: the most remote end of Jordan Pond. The spot we meet at is secluded, and other shifters acknowledge it as *our* spot, too--even though it's within the neutral territory of the national park.

Once we've shifted, as a group, we'll be meeting with the conclave. Shawn, Harris, Kevin and Jamie won't have the ability to change into their bear forms since we've got them all locked up in the shed and out of sight of the full moon.

It's getting darker and I feel the change beginning to crackle through my bones. At any other time, I have to consciously call it up, but during the full moon, it happens almost without my will; any shifters outside, under the moon, are the affected the same. The full moon change is always a big one: apart from being nearly involuntary, it feels like the purest of transformations, where we're more truly aligned with the animal parts of our consciousness.

The rest of my clan is beginning to look as restless as I am. I can feel their expectations; I can hear it in their minds. We need to resolve this issue and restore harmony to Acadia--and honor the lives of Matilda and Harold by bringing these assholes to justice once and for all.

I spot the members of the conclave approaching my clan's territory, all of them looking appropriately cautious about entering. There are five of them: Jeremy, an older bear; a mountain lioness named Vanessa; Leonard, a wolf who's only a few years older than I am; a she-wolf named Priscilla, and Nathan, a fox. Every five years, the shifters in the area surrounding our neutral territory hold an election to appoint a new conclave, which is meant to represent as many of the different shifter groups as possible.

"Good evening, Knox," Jeremy says as they approach, stopping just outside the border of our territory. "You asked us to oversee an issue with some outsiders disrupting the peace?"

"Yes, I did," I say, beckoning them to enter. They cross over the scent-marked boundary of our clan's territory, which distinguishes the area from the rest of the park, and advance towards our group.

"Tell us what the situation is, and then we will hear from the accused," Vanessa says.

"There are actually several incidents I'd like to recount for you. A few days ago, these bears--who have been causing trouble regularly for weeks, since the last full moon when they arrived--were on the verge of attacking a human visiting the park before I caught them and sent them on their way. The person was a journalist; their acts could have exposed us all if she was able to get away from them and they weren't able control their feral sides."

"This is serious, indeed," Jeremy agrees.

I nod. "They tried to attack again the following

day in their bear forms. I got into a brawl with one of them in an attempt to keep them from going after a nearby human."

"I see," says Jeremy. "Is there anything else you'd like to add?"

"I would, and this is the worst offense of them all." I motion to Trent, who's standing to my left, "He found evidence that at least one of the four did, in fact, murder two bears from my clan, Matilda and Harold. Shawn, the alpha of their crew, left his scent-marks all over their bodies, which Trent found a ways north of here tonight."

The members of the conclave nod, looking grave.

"We'd like to extend our sincere condolences to each of you," Nathan says, as the rest of the conclave bows their heads in agreement. "We need to speak to the accused now, and we must do it quickly. Where are they being detained?"

"They're in a shed nearby, over on the edge of our territory," I tell them, gesturing in the direction of the trail leading to where the delinquents are.

"Very well. We'll head down to hear their pleas, and we should be back shortly to discuss the verdict," Nathan says.

I nod. "We appreciate your help very much."

As they leave, I look up at the sky, feeling the tingling through my body intensify. The moon will be out within a matter of minutes, and we will all need to transform into our other forms. I take a deep breath, holding the change at bay by force of will. I sniff the air--I can almost smell the magic that makes the change possible, dancing through the little secluded spot by the pond.

The members of my clan begin to prepare themselves for the change as soon as the moon rises. I hold off, not wanting to commit to the shift until I hear from the conclave, and I look around, taking deep breaths.

My focus shifts to Hannah for a moment as I await their return. *I'm 35 years old; at this point in my life, I need to get serious about finding my mate; someone to settle down and have cubs with*, I tell myself. *But if Hannah finds out what I really am, there's zero chance of having a future like that with her. Not to mention she isn't even from around here; it'd be hard to convince her to move up to these parts and abandon everything she's been doing with her life up until now.*

I'm plucked from my thoughts as I my ears pick up on rustling within the tall grass nearby. The conclave is making their way back toward the pond, and their expressions are somber. Behind them, Shawn, Harris, Kevin and Jamie trudge along, bound in silver chains; we made sure to take that precaution once we'd managed to track them down for the second time, not wanting to risk having them escape again.

"We've come to a decision," Vanessa says, looking first at me, then over to the rest of the clan. "This is neutral territory, and it's indisputable that these four have violated the terms of being on this land, and what it means to all of us. But one of the tenets of our society is that even wrongdoers are allowed to attempt to defend themselves in combat."

This isn't the result I was hoping for, but I know I have to abide by it. "So, what has the conclave concluded?"

As I look at the five members, Jeremy is the one to speak up. "At moonrise, the four guilty members will shift, and they will be given a twenty-minute head start, at which point, they will be fair game. If they can escape the territory before the Alpha can reach them, they'll earn their freedom. If they are able to successfully conquer the Alpha, they'll receive their freedom as well. But, let it be known, any confrontation will be fought to the death. If they manage to earn their freedom and attempt to re-enter the territory at any given time, execution sentences will be carried out without hesitation."

"To make our point clear, absolutely no one may intervene," Vanessa adds. "It is between the Alpha, Knox Bernard, and these four."

The verdict is better than what I had been dreading, but not by much. I'll have to chase down four separate bears; if they have any sense at all, they'll take off in different directions. I'll have to take them all out separately if I want to make sure that they will never threaten me, my clan, or Hannah again.

"I accept," I say, because frankly, I don't have a choice.

"Take the chains off these four, and we will oversee the challenge," Jeremy says.

Trent and Cassidy step forward and begin to remove the chains binding Harris, Shawn, Jamie, and Kevin.

I move closer to Shawn and a low growl escapes from my throat. "Why? Why did you do it?"

Shawn smirks, still bound by his chains. "Do *what*, pussy boy?"

I level my eyes with his. "You know damn well what I'm talking about, jerk-off!" My growl is now a deep roar at this point.

"Oh, those old geezers? Please, I was doing you a favor." He spits in my face. "Survival of the fittest, motherfucker."

I lunge for his throat, but Trent and Alex pull me back.

"You'll have plenty of time to settle this in a few minutes," Trent reminds me.

Shawn laughs maniacally, shaking so violently from his hysterics that his chains clatter through the night air. "We'll see about that," he snickers as Alex steps behind Shawn and frees him.

I breathe deeply, trying to calm myself as I start stripping out of my clothes. I feel the magic of the change intensifying in me, the animal instincts rising up to take control of my mind more completely than they do at any other time of the month. I give into it, closing my eyes, letting the transformation course through my whole body, from head to toe.

I feel my heart nearly push through my ribcage as I'm taken over by the seismic change. Tremors ripple through my limbs as my joints and bones begin to crack and morph violently. I feel my face elongate, stretching into a broad snout as I begin to taste iron-rich blood, my razor-sharp ursine teeth now emerging from my jaws. My eyes involuntarily roll to the back of my skull as equal doses of pain and ecstasy flow through my entire being. My skin tears and gives way to accommodate the lengthening of my bones, and tufts of thick, black fur force their way to the surface in its place. A moment later, I've made my full transformation.

When I open my eyes again I'm a black bear, surrounded by the other black bears of my clan, and the members of the conclave in their animal forms: a fox, a mountain lioness, two wolves, and a grizzly bear.

The grizzly, Jeremy, lets out a deep bellow, and I see Shawn and his accomplices lumber off into the woods next to the pond, dispersing to take advantage of their twenty-minute head start. Despite my animal form, there's just enough of my human mind still persisting for me to hold back and keep myself from automatically chasing after the four.

I wait impatiently, counting the seconds in my mind. Before I can hunt or forage for the foods I love, before I can commune with the rest of my clan, I have to take care of this problem. At least it'll all be over soon; one way or another, the four shitheads will be out of my life for good by the end of the night.

To pass the time, I sniff the night air, reading the scents painted through it. There's a new hive of bees not far from the lake, and I look forward to raiding it sometime soon after dark when they'll be less defensive. I also want to make sure to get the last berries of the season to share with Hannah.

It's almost time, and I'm sniffing the air again to try and determine which path to take first when I catch her scent. It's unmistakable: lavender honey with a deeper musk underneath; delicious, magnetic and so fresh that it has to mean that Hannah is close by, right now. It's not an old scent from her possibly tromping through the area earlier in the day; I would have noticed it before.

Adrenaline shoots through me and the entire situation immediately becomes drastically more complicated. I have to wonder if she saw me--and the clan, and the conclave--change forms. These four reckless deviants pose a serious threat to Hannah if I can't get to them in time. I lower my head and let out a bellow. My human mind wants to take over--this situation is too complicated--but my animal mind maintains control. The simplest thoughts I have dominate my brain: protect the female, and remove the threat.

I take off after one of the scent trails, keeping part of my mind on the fact that Hannah is in the woods, too; I need to keep away from her, if I can. What is she even doing in this part of the woods at night? *Not important. Get the assholes taken down first and worry about that later.*

I follow Harris' trail, keeping myself aware of the others; as I suspected, they seem to have all gone off in different directions. At least, if I can track them down and take out two of them, the other two will be barred from the park for the rest of their lives. That would be a start.

Just as I'm getting close to Harris, though, I catch Hannah's scent again, and then, as I'm sniffing the air and the ground, I realize that Shawn's scent has crossed into this area of the woods, too; he's been through the trail in the last fifteen minutes, to judge by the freshness of the scent. I hear a scream, and my animal and human brains identify it immediately.

It's Hannah.

I quickly abandon any thought of going after Harris. Instinct takes over. I have to protect Hannah, whatever she's run afoul of; I can only suspect that it's Shawn.

I sniff the air and I find the direction Hannah is headed in, and a moment later, I find her, just yards away from me. She screams again, and I'm running towards her before I realize what I'm doing.

CHAPTER THIRTEEN
HANNAH

I don't know what I was expecting to see when I hiked out to one of the suspicious sites I'd noticed while cross-referencing the maps, but it definitely wasn't *this*.

A group of people--including my most recent sex partner, Knox--stripped naked, and then somehow, violating every natural law, disappeared into the bodies of a bunch of bears, along with a fox, two wolves, and of all things, a goddamn mountain lion.

Whatever other plans I had for the night evaporate from my head completely as I watch four of the bears shuffle off into the woods in a hurry. One of the others chases after him and I fumble with my phone, doing my best to capture this all on video while still trying to get over the initial shock of what I'd seen. I decide that it would be a moot point to try and check out whatever other sites I'd mapped out. Jessica was right after all; there's some fucking freaky shit happening in these parts, and there's no way I'm going to stay in the park with these roaming bands of human-animal creatures running around.

But then, as I attempt to find my way back toward my car, I lose the trail, and then get lost in the park altogether, with my phone now out of range of a cell tower.

It's bad enough to be wandering through the woods, unable to find my way out as the temperature continues to drop, but when I hear a growl from a few yards away and the barely-there sound of leaves and sticks crunching, I somehow know--immediately--that I'm the target of the animal in question.

My heart pounds in my chest as I try to figure out what to do about the situation. I hear myself screaming, one high, loud yelp escaping my throat, but I almost don't know how it could be me; I'm so removed from my own body.

I can't stop moving, but I force myself to slow down to avoid tripping over something and leave myself sprawling in the scrub, a perfect little bundle of tasty human meat that's just waiting to be devoured.

Is it one of the people that turned into an animal? Is it Knox? Something tells me that it's definitely not Knox; he wouldn't be chasing after me...frightening me...would he? How much humanity stays in the mind of the animal after he or she transforms?

I get a mental flashback of the sight of about thirty or more humans, standing stark naked near a lake in the woods, almost seeming to dissolve as more and more animalistic characteristics come over them. *As for the wolves, I guess you'd have to call them werewolves, wouldn't you? But what would you call a human that changes into a mountain lion, or a bear?*

I try to shake off the panic and shock I'm feeling when I hear the telltale sounds of a heavy, large predator behind me. I scream again without even realizing it until my strained throat forces me to cough. It's moving fast and I need to figure out what I'm going to do; I can't just keep walking like an idiot. I reach into my bag; I have a hunting knife that Mary gave me when I told her I was going to be checking out a few different parts of the woods at night. She'd pointed out that while it's technically a crime to kill animals in the park, I could maim one in self-defense and not get charged, and more to the point, it would be better to deal with criminal charges than to die a gruesome death.

I take the knife out and turn around to face the animal coming toward me. There's enough moonlight for me to catch a few glimpses of the creature as it descends on me: it's a huge bear with tattered, mangy fur. *Okay, so that bear from the other day...* My brain does rapid calculus as the bear barrels down on me and I realize that the massive, glorious-looking bear that I'd seen fighting with this other one--when I hadn't been able to find Knox--had to have *been* Knox. That explains the bear fight from the other day, the missing jacket and, more importantly, how quickly Knox had gotten back to me. Everything fell into place.

But before I have time to make sense of that revelation, the bear is within fighting distance. I take the knife and hold it up threateningly. "I know you're a human, or part human," I say. I try to stand as strong as I can and attempt to make eye contact with the leering, growling beast. "If you come at me, I'm going to do my level best to kill you." Surely, these shapeshifting, human-animal people aren't protected by the park's regulations. What happens to *them* when they die? Do they remain in their animal forms, or turn back to humans?

The bear hesitates for a moment, seems to size me up, and then lunges at me. I lash out with the knife, but before I can even get at the bear, I hear crashing and a roar nearby. I hear someone--or something--coming at us, and then the bear that was about to attack me is on his side, bowled over by another bear.

I stagger back, stunned at what I'm witnessing. The two bears go at it immediately, swiping at each other, snapping their teeth and growling, wrestling on the ground as each of them struggles to gain the upper hand.

It takes me a few moments to realize that the bear who's come to my rescue is actually Knox; he must have recognized my scream and came running. I'm torn between relief and new fear, and once again, I have to wonder how much of humanity is in the bear that's pounding on the one that would have attacked me in a few seconds? Is it the human inside that made Knox come to my rescue, or some animal instinct based on my scent and the sound of my voice?

I suddenly lose my bearings and fall to the ground, hard enough to make my teeth click and my jaw hurt from the impact, and I see the battle continue to rage on. It's like a weirdly-tinted deja vu from the other day, and while part of me is aware of the possibility that I might still get attacked, my body's frozen as my mind is working through the surrealness of the situation. Reality slaps me in the face as it fully occurs to me that yes, I truly did see Knox--a man I'd had sex with, and more than once--transform into a fucking bear. And now that bear is protecting me from another bear, who apparently wants to attack me, for reasons of its own.

All at once, I come back to myself as I hear a sickening crunch and a roar. I look around and spot the two furry forms on the ground, and for a second, I don't know what happened. I've been in a state of complete shock, so enveloped in my own thoughts that I totally lost track of what was going on in front of me.

The larger of the two bears--Knox, in his other form--rises, and the other bear doesn't move at all. I realize, with a sickening feeling in my stomach, that Knox killed the other bear. I should be grateful, and a part of me is, but I'm also horrified.

Knox-bear lumbers towards me slowly, snuffling and making low noises in his throat. I have no idea what to say. I have no idea what to even *think*. Is Knox even really in there? The bear stops short of me and lets out a groan, and I stagger back on my ass, scrambling on the ground with my hands, unable to even muster the mental capacity to stand up and run.

Before my eyes, Knox-bear seems to shrink, shift and move, and I realize that he's transforming back into a human, albeit very slowly. It seems almost painful; the sound of bones cracking and joints popping back into place send a chill down my spine.

Then, finally, Knox is standing in front of me, fully naked but fully human, streaked with blood but with only a handful of scratches over him.

"So," he says, his voice low. He coughs. "I take it you saw something."

"You're...some kind of...bear...shapeshifter," I say, shaking my head. "But that's impossible."

"It's obviously possible," Knox counters. "You just saw me shift with your own eyes." He gives me a wry grin. "I'd hoped you didn't see the first change, but when I heard you tell Shawn here..." he kicks at the bear, which seems to be melting into a human, which is somehow even more unnerving than Knox's transformation, "that you knew he was human, I figured if I could get rid of him, that would be a good time to come clean."

"Thanks, I guess," I say, still numb and stunned from the whole ordeal.

"It's a lot to take in." Knox looks worried.

I smile weakly. "Yeah...it is," I agree. "I just found out that not only are shapeshifters actually a thing, but that I've had sex with one more than once without even knowing."

"Who knows, you might have slept with one before me," Knox says. "We're sworn to secrecy about it."

I mentally scan through the last few guys I've dated. "Nope. I highly doubt it."

"You'd never know..."

I furrow my brow at that. "So... this is why you wanted to wait a couple of days to see me again," I say, remembering that tidbit. "*This* is why you were going to be busy." I'd figured on any number of outlandish scenarios, but this is one I never could have foreseen. "So, what, is the park some kind of hunting ground for your group?"

"It's not only for my group, but any shifter who wants to come here. As long as they're willing to obey the rules." Knox gestures absently to the dead bear-man, who now looks completely like a man, and a naked one at that. "He and three others broke the rules when they tried to attack you, and when they tried to fight me on the premises. This one here even killed a few of my friends."

"He...and three others..." It hits me then: the four men who tried to attack me on my first visit were all part bear. More of the whole crazy story falls into place in my mind. They were also the bears that had interrupted my picnic with Knox the second time I came to the park. And now at least one of them was dead.

"I...I think I need to get back to Mary's," I say. "I have a lot to think about."

"Will you come see me before you leave? And I think--I hope--you're not going to write about this, are you?" Knox looks more worried than ever. "It would put my entire kind in jeopardy."

"I need to think this through before I decide what I'm going to do."

I give myself a shake. Questions start up in my brain; on and on, the significance of what I've just learned in the last hour or so renders itself to a bunch of trivial nonsense.

"So, can we meet up like we were originally planning to? How about that?"

I think about it, and in spite of the shock I feel about what I've learned, I have to admit that I'm curious. Knox didn't hurt me, after all; he saved my life.

"It's a deal," I say. "Now if I can just get the hell out of here…"

"I'll show you the way, but then I'll have to get back to hunting the other bears down," Knox says. The phrase sends a shiver down my spine, but I don't ask any more questions.

CHAPTER FOURTEEN
KNOX

I'm not sure that I'm exactly holding my breath, but at the same time, I'm determined not to be disappointed if Hannah doesn't show up.

I'd hoped to keep her from finding out about my bear side--for the time being, anyway--but now that she knows, I need to find a way to keep her from spilling our secret. Above and beyond that, though, I need to see her again. The way I reacted to knowing she was in danger, in my animal form, told me a lot. The fact that I was able to shift back to human form during the full moon told me even more. With Shawn now dead and the other three bears off the territory for good, I finally felt it was safe to have Hannah back here.

When I see her walking towards my cabin from the front of the park, I feel a wave of relief. If nothing else, she's agreed to see me, and she looks interested instead of frightened or shocked. I take a deep breath and steady myself. Just because she agreed to come, just because she's willing to talk to me, doesn't mean that she's interested in anything more. And I have to be prepared for that.

"Hey," Hannah says as she steps up to me.

"How have you been?"

Hannah raises her eyebrows. "I've had a lot to process," she admits. She kicks at some loose mulch on the trail leading up to my cabin and looks up, meeting my gaze. "I've given it a lot of thought. It's unethical for me to not publish the truth, but sometimes in this field, you have to balance ethics with what is truly the right thing to do," she says. "I mean, if I published the truth, most people would just think that I've lost my mind. But, if even a fringe element ended up actually believing me, surely a witch hunt would ensue that would put you and your kind in grave danger. I can't and won't take that risk." She shakes her head. "I'll just have to write something else."

"Well, you could still write about the park," I suggest. "Just not about the angle that includes people like me."

Hannah chuckles. "Let's go inside and talk," she tells me, and I'm only too ready to agree.

We go into my cabin and I offer her something to drink. "I'll have a cup of coffee," she says, and I pour one for her, bringing milk and sugar to the table to go with it.

"Well, I'm sure you have a lot of questions. Where should we start?"

It seems so stilted, so awkward between us now, and I hate it.

"Can... can you turn someone else into a bear, or whatever you are, by biting them?"

I shake my head. "No, it's something you're born with," I reply.

"I see," she says, stirring a little more sugar into her coffee. "So... is a shifter baby born as a human, or an animal?"

"Really, it could go either way," I tell her. "If the mother is a shifter and she's in her animal form as she gives birth, the baby will be born in his or her animal state. If she's in her human form, she'll give birth to an infant in his or her human state," I explain. "It also depends on whether or not one of the parents is a full-blooded human."

"Wait a second, so humans and shifters are capable of producing offspring together?"

"They can. Their children would have at least a 50% chance of becoming shifters. Even if they didn't end up becoming shifters, they would carry the gene. If they mate with other shifters one day, they'd have children who could shift," I explain.

"Wow, sounds complicated." She takes another sip from her mug before asking, "Have...you ever had sex in your bear form?"

I nod. "Only with another werebear, never with a human or an actual bear," I say.

"Okay, so *werebear* is the term you like to use. Well, what is the connection between your status as a human and your status as a werebear?"

"I became the Alpha male of the bear pack that is technically the host for this territory when I became the administrator," I say.

"Do you have to have a partner to be an Alpha male?"

I shake my head. "No, but it helps," I admit. "I've been waiting to meet the right person before I choose my mate."

I pause for a moment and decide that now's as good of a time as any to cut the bullshit and tell her what's on my mind; what's been on my mind for days now. "If I'm being honest..." I say, taking her hands in mine, "I think that person is you."

Hannah's eyes widen for a moment. "What makes you think I'd be a good *mate*?"

I gently take her face in the palms of my hands and look into those gorgeous hazel eyes of hers. "Hannah, I knew I wanted you from the first time I met you," I tell her. "Every time we got together after that, I knew it even more strongly. And the other night, well, that confirmed it."

"How do you know for sure?" she asks.

I smile slowly. "My bear side tells me you smell

like something that should be mine," I tell her. "Like something I should protect and devote myself to; something I should take care of."

She stares out the window for the next few minutes, pondering over it all, but then she cracks a small smile.

"You know, I'd be lying if I told you I haven't felt something between us; something strong that's more than just..." She looks down for a moment, but then her gaze returns to mine. "It's like I *need* you, Knox, and no matter what the rational side of my brain screams out to me, there's something inside that tells me..."

"That we're meant to be together?"

"Yes," she says. "I know that, in many ways, we're so different, but if I just go home and try to forget this ever happened--that we ever happened—I know I'll regret it." She reaches over to the table to grasp my hands, "I have to see where this will go."

This is promising indeed, but I try to press her further to make sure we're on the same page. "Do you mean in terms of me living here and you living back in Boston?"

Hannah shrugs. "It would depend, I guess. It's probably against the rules for an Alpha to get involved with someone who's not...like you, right?"

"We Alphas make a lot of our own rules," I say.

"Isn't that going to piss off some of the others?" Hannah looks dubious.

"Everyone knows and respects that the Alpha lives by his or her own rules, so no. Besides, I've never heard of any Alpha being tried by a conclave for choosing a human as his or her mate."

She looks at me for a long moment. "All I ask, for the time being, is for you to be patient with me, Knox. This is a lot to take in, and there's a lot to adjust to."

I think about it; in all my musings, in all my hopes, I haven't thought through what I would do if Hannah would actually entertain the thought of being with me.

"I'm willing to do whatever it takes to make this work," I say.

I keep looking at her for a long moment. Being so close to her again, breathing in her scent, I think about what it would be like to be with her--to have her as my mate--for the rest of my life, and it makes my heart feel like it could explode right out of my chest. *I just have to make sure to give her a little breathing room.*

"Well, I'll have to head back home in a few days," she says. "Why don't I get clearance from my boss to work remotely, and I'll come back up and we can spend a little more time getting to know each other here in the cabin? That's one of the perks of my job; I can pretty much work wherever there's a Wi-Fi signal. How does that sound?" Hannah sits back slightly in her chair and raises an eyebrow.

"That sounds like a perfect start," I say with a grin. "No matter how much time you need back home, I'll be here waiting for you."

All the awkwardness leaves us then, and we're talking about the future like nothing strange at all stands in our way. The idea of lunch goes out the window completely. When Hannah gets up to put her coffee mug in my sink, I grab her and pull her into my lap, kissing her, tasting the sweetened coffee on her lips.

We immediately begin working at each other's clothes, almost tearing them, and I know--deep down--that it's only a matter of time before she'll be living up here with me in my cabin.

I put my mouth to work, dipping down to Hannah's tits and claiming them, worshipping them with my lips and tongue as I manage to get her panties off and toss them across the room.

Hannah squirms in my lap, and I can feel her wet heat against my throbbing, aching cock, like our bodies are doing everything they can to merge as one. I fall completely into instinct, getting the last of Hannah's clothes off and lifting her up onto the kitchen table. I work my way down from her tits to her pussy, and it's so deliciously soaking wet, so hot and ready for me, that I can't even bring myself to wait or to tease Hannah. I push her gently onto her back and bury my face against her slick folds, sliding my tongue up and down, tasting her hungrily.

Hannah moans out and the sound is like music to my ears, spurring me on as I work her with my lips and tongue. I spread her legs wide and bring the tip of my tongue up to her clit, swirling it in tight circles before dipping down to her entrance, sucking as much of her into my mouth as I can. I bring her to the edge of climax in a matter of moments and then back off, slowing down just enough to let her cool down. Over and over again, I get her so hot that I know she can barely stand it and then I stop just short of letting her get what she really wants, until I know she thinks she's going to die if I don't let her come.

I pull back finally and look at her face; she's flushed and panting, looking almost like an animal herself, and I love her more than I ever thought possible, but I know it's not the time to tell her. I have to wait for her to feel the same way; for her to feel comfortable saying it.

The animal in me wants to flip her onto her stomach, but I know I need to be as human as possible around her--for now, at least. I wrap her legs around my waist and guide the tip of my cock against her soaking wet folds, and thrust into her, taking her all at once.

We fall into a rhythm immediately, with Hannah pushing her hips down, twisting them in reaction to my movements, and it feels so completely perfect that I know she has to feel it, too. I start slow and then gradually build up speed, holding myself back as I bring Hannah to the edge yet again--but this time I let her tumble over it and ride through her orgasm, kissing her face everywhere and dipping down to her tits. I manage to hold my own climax back throughout Hannah's, and slow down while she's recovering, moving just enough to keep her going while I maintain my own arousal.

Then we're moving together again, speeding up, and the feeling of Hannah's muscles clenching around me in little spasms is almost more than I can take, in a matter of mere moments. But I keep it together, working up her arousal, turning her on more and more. I take advantage of the lull to worship her tits, her lips, to touch her sensitive little clit, working her until she's so turned on it must be killing her and then slamming into her with all I've got when my need gets the better of me.

The second time I feel her body clench around me in orgasm, I tumble into my own climax, coming harder than I ever have with anyone else. I groan against Hannah's chest, against her shoulder, and kiss her as wave after wave of pleasure washes over me, and I feel that connection between us, that bond that I know only happens when a bear--or any shifter--has found his or her mate.

I sag against Hannah, panting for breath, and I feel her body fluttering around me in erratic little post-orgasmic spasms as aftershocks work through her.

"Weren't...weren't we going to get lunch?"

I laugh at Hannah's question. "Feeling hungry?"

Hannah nods. "I could eat a horse," she tells me. I breathe in the smell of her; just knowing that gorgeous, intoxicating scent is going to be in my life permanently--even if Hannah doesn't fully realize it yet--is enough to make me want to shift and run through the park's grounds, roaring my triumph.

I pull myself back and grin down at the woman I've fallen for. "I'm all out of horse, but I do have a fresh wild duck and some fingerling potatoes and carrots that I'd love to roast up for you," I say with a wink. "My family has a recipe that's been handed down for generations that I've been dying to make for you. Let me get that started, then afterwards...maybe we could move the party to the bedroom."

"That sounds amazing," Hannah says. "I vote yes."

I slip on my boxers and head to the kitchen to start preparing our meal. Fifteen minutes later, just as I'm putting the duck in the oven, Hannah's just gotten out of the shower and joins me, wearing nothing but one of my flannels.

"Hey, I just thought of something...something about the research I'd been doing."

I laugh, "Does your mind ever stop?"

Hannah gives me a playful shove. "No seriously," she says. "So, remember how I wasn't able to find the birth certificates for some of Acadia's founders?"

I look up from the cutting board, where I'd been chopping garlic to add to the gravy. "Yeah?"

"Well, how long have shifters been gathering in Acadia for?"

I pause mid-chop. She'd seen my clan and the concave shift right there before her eyes, so there was no denying the *existence* of shifters. But the histories of Acadia and the NPS? I took a sacred oath, vowing to never reveal the true reason behind how they came to be.

"Shifters have been around just as long as humans have."

"You should be a politician," she says, crossing her arms as she laughs. "I asked how long have they been *gathering in Acadia* for."

"Oh, I don't know. A long time."

"Well, I put two and two together and had the thought that perhaps some of those founders were shifters themselves," she says.

"Is that so?" I stiffen, trying to act as nonchalant as possible, but then remember that I hadn't let her in on the secret; she's a smart woman, and was able to piece the puzzle together herself.

"Am I right, or am I right?" she asks, grabbing a piece of carrot from the cutting board to munch on.

I grin. "Well, what makes you think that?"

"I concocted the idea that if, say, one of the founder's mothers gave birth in her animal form, the founder would have been born as an animal...and what wild animal would have a birth certificate?"

I hand her another piece of carrot. "That's pretty farfetched, don't you think?"

She laughs. "Um, if you'd asked me last week about the concept of a bunch of naked humans morphing into animals under the full moon, I would have told you *that's* farfetched. So, am I on to something here?"

I turn around, grabbing her by the waist as I pull her in close for a kiss. "I'll never tell."

"Well, what if I phrase it this way: am I crazy, or am I smart?"

"You," I say, planting a trail of kisses down her neck, "are the smartest person I've ever known."

And she *is*. How I got so lucky to find a woman as irresistible as Hannah, I'll never know. For the first time in my life, I notice the unrelenting drive of my inner bear relax, creating harmony between my dual sides like I've never experienced. It knows I've found my destined mate, and even though things between Hannah and I are just getting started, at this rate, my instincts tell me that she'll be pregnant within the year.

THE END

ABOUT THE AUTHOR

Meg Ripley is an author of erotic science fiction and paranormal romance stories. As a child, she had recurring dreams about being abducted by aliens and has been obsessed with extraterrestrial life ever since. A Seattle native, Meg can often be found curled up in a local coffee house with her laptop.

Download Meg's entire *Caught Between Dragons* series when you sign up for her newsletter!

Sign up by visiting Meg's Facebook page: https://www.facebook.com/authormegripley/

www.ingramcontent.com/pod-product-compliance
Lightning Source LLC
LaVergne TN
LVHW040053110625
813568LV00030B/326